Fielder's Choice

Also by Michael Bowen

Can't Miss
Badger Game
Washington Deceased

Fielder's Choice

MICHAEL
BOWEN

St. Martin's Press   New York

Fielder's Choice is a work of fiction. Except for well-known historical events and personages, the events described did not happen, and the characters depicted do not exist. Any apparent similarity between episodes in *Fielder's Choice* and events that actually did take place, or between characters appearing in the story and actual persons, living or dead, is purely coincidental and is not intended.

NOTE TO READER: Careful readers with long memories will note that certain liberties have been taken in *Fielder's Choice* with the schedule of the 1962 National League Championship Baseball Season. This has been done for a variety of technical reasons, all of them good and none of them worth taking up the reader's time with extended discussion.

Production Editor: David Stanford Burr

Design by Judy Dannecker

Library of Congress Cataloging-in-Publication Data

Bowen, Michael,
        Fielder's choice / Michael Bowen.
                p.   cm.
        ISBN 0-312-05850-0
        I. Title.
        PS3552.0864F5 1991
        813'.54—dc20   90-27417
                                                                                    CIP

First Edition: June 1991

10   9   8   7   6   5   4   3   2   1

To P.G., in appreciation

FIELDER'S CHOICE is the act of a fielder who handles a fair grounder and, instead of throwing to first base to put out the batter-runner, throws to another base in an attempt to put out a preceding runner.

OFFICIAL BASEBALL RULES, REVISED EDITION, SECTION 2.00 AT 7 (1989)

Before September 26

1

Chapter One

Going into the sixth inning of the New York Mets' game against the Milwaukee Braves on September 26, 1962, Jerry Fielder figured that the Mets still had a decent chance to win. As it turned out, that was the last mistake Fielder ever made.

The following afternoon, just before four o'clock, Sandrine Cadette Curry got out of the bath she had just finished and began to dry herself with unhurried strokes of a thick, burgundy terrycloth towel. She was twenty-four years old, with blue-black hair, a smooth, brown, Latin complexion, and classic Mediterranean features—until you got to her eyes. Her eyes were royal blue, the triumph of the Norman genes she carried along with those from southern France.

When Sandy had finished drying herself off, she slipped into a robe that matched the towel and walked back into the bedroom she shared with Thomas Andrew Curry. She started to whistle, then checked herself because she didn't want to wake Thomas up if he still needed sleep. The two of them hadn't gotten to bed until around 9:30 that morning.

Even though she had by now been married for some three months to a man with plenty of money, Sandy still had a full-time job. Four o'clock on a workday afternoon would usually have found her busy at the office rather than relaxing in the Eastside apartment she and Thomas called home. A lot of things about the last twenty-four hours had been out of the ordinary, though.

She knelt gingerly on the bed, rather close to her recumbent husband, and examined him knowingly. His eyes were closed lightly, his breathing regular but not deep. With the upper backs of the fingers of her right hand she brushed his right cheek, from the ear to the tip of the brown moustache, scratching over the abrasive stubble of a day-and-a-half's beard growth.

He stirred slightly. She smiled. Bending over, she kissed his neck just where it joined his shoulder.

"Thomas," she said, surveying him from head to foot as she spoke, "you are either awake or you are having a dream in which I had better be playing a featured role."

"Mmmf," Thomas said. His eyes half opened. "I dreamed you took that robe off."

She smiled again and began to do so. His eyes opened all the way.

"Here, let me help you with that," he said.

Then the phone rang.

"We can ignore that," she said. "Push the button that turns it off."

Thomas's hand reached for the receiver instead of the button.

"Do not dare," Sandy commanded him. She bit him on the point of his shoulder.

"You're going to get bitten back if you keep that up, Mrs. Curry," Thomas said.

4

"Promises, promises."

The phone rang again.

"Thomas—"

"Sandy, precious, one of the things that separates us from the lower animals is the ability to control our appetites."

"Thomas," Sandy said eagerly, "I *adore* when you talk like a Protestant." She kissed him hungrily on the throat.

Thomas mashed a button below the phone's rotary dial, aborting the third ring in mid-jangle.

"Now, then," Thomas said, "what you have coming is one bite, and—"

The phone rang again, the ring this time long and insistent. This meant that it came from the doorman downstairs and that he thought it was very important.

"Listen, Joe," Thomas groaned into the receiver after snatching it up, "please tell whoever it is . . . What? . . . Who? . . . Yes, we're acquainted with Jerry Fielder . . . What do you mean 'were'? . . . I see. All right, yes, come right up."

His last two sentences had been spoken more slowly than his first hurried words, and when he turned back to Sandy after replacing the receiver Thomas's face was suddenly quiet and subdued.

"That was a policeman," Thomas said, "a detective. Someone killed Jerry Fielder during the game last night."

Chapter Two

For a few weeks after September 26, I thought occasionally about whether I was responsible for Fielder's death. I don't mean morally, I mean causally responsible, in the technical, legal sense: But for Theodore Furst and what he did and didn't do that day and night, would Jerry Fielder still be alive?

The first answer I came up with was, who cares? That generally stopped satisfying me about halfway through the second martini. Two was my limit, so I ended up probing the question a bit more thoroughly.

I finally concluded that the answer was no. The junior partner at the small law firm known as Curry & Furst wasn't the proximate cause of Jerry Fielder's death.

The story of how I reached that conclusion involves Thomas and Sandy, two people I like quite a lot. Sandy worked full-time for me, translating cables and correspondence from my German and Francophone clients, organizing my paperwork, and doing anything else my carefully nurtured international practice required. Thomas, on the other hand, freelanced. I could get his help on specific projects, but he wasn't my employee, or the firm's, or anybody else's.

I got most of this story from them, bits at a time, years later, over everything from Chardonnay and oysters Rockefeller to ham sandwiches and beer. It starts at a baseball game about three weeks before the last game Jerry Fielder ever saw.

"Is he out, Thomas?"

"No, he's on base."

"Even though he failed to hit the ball?"

"That's right. He got a walk." Blank look. "A base on balls. A free pass. The right to go to first base without a play being made on him."

"Why do they call it a walk?"

"Because since no play could be made on him he could literally walk to the base if he wanted to."

"Then why is he running?"

"He needs the exercise, I suppose."

"Thomas," Sandy said then, as Richie Ashburn stepped up for the Mets, "if I ask you something will you promise to answer me seriously?" Her lilting French accent, always noticeable, was even more pronounced than usual that September because she and Thomas had just spent most of their honeymoon in France.

"Of course. I'm never frivolous about baseball."

"I have noticed, I think. My question is this: Is baseball objectivist or phenomenological?"

"I don't have the faintest idea."

"I mean to ask, is there truly a coherent principle informing what the players do, or are they simply engaging in random movements, with spectators investing what happens with their own subjective meanings?"

"Sandy, I'm not altogether sure that was a serious question."

"You mustn't say that, Thomas. To be amusing Americans must avoid cynicism."

"Perhaps the game is too subtle for the European mind."

"That must be it," Sandy nodded, Gallic irony richly coloring each syllable. "I am nonetheless trying to grasp it."

"And well you should. The United States has made four unique contributions to world culture: jazz, peanut butter, representative democracy, and baseball. As a resident alien and future citizen, you should be familiar with all of them."

"I will do my best," Sandy promised solemnly as Ashburn singled.

Thomas shouldn't have been surprised that introducing Sandy to baseball was turning out to be a challenge. Baseball is utterly unlike other widely popular sports. You can't pick up its essentials at a glance the first time you see a game. You have to assimilate baseball patiently, ideally at an impressionable age.

For baseball resonates most reliably against the unalloyed metals of childhood memory. When Bobby Thomson hit his dramatic ninth-inning home run to put the Giants into the 1951 World Series instead of the Dodgers, when Dusty Rhodes hit the first pinch-hit home run in World Series history, when Willie Mays made his unbelievable, back-to-the-plate, over-the-shoulder, running-full-tilt catch of Vic Wertz's mammoth drive to dead center field—all of those things happened at the Polo Grounds in the fifties—they evoked in Thomas and me and ten million like us memories we had grown up on, of Carl Hubbell and Ducky Medwick and a time when there were sixteen teams in all the major leagues and three of those teams played in New York. This was something that Sandy couldn't even dimly imagine.

It didn't help that the home team at the Polo Grounds in 1962 wasn't the Giants, who had decamped to San Francisco and were on their way to a pennant, but a decrepit travesty called the New York Mets. Nineteen sixty-two was the year the Mets broke in. They were terrible.

Marv Throneberry was coming up. Thomas sensed that another attempt by Sandy to reduce the national pastime to a rigorously logical Cartesian construct might also be coming up, and he moved to forestall it.

"I'm going for a beer," he said. "Would you like one?"

"That would be lovely," Sandy said.

Before Thomas could get up, a voice from behind them called out, "R.J., go get two beers for these folks."

Thomas and Sandy turned around in their seats as a tall, muscular, black-haired young man scurried toward the concessionaires. Still seated was the freckled redhead in his midthirties who had issued this instruction. He was wearing a white, button-down, oxford cloth dress shirt, no tie, a pair of faded Levi's blue jeans, white tube socks, Keds all-court canvas shoes that had once been white, and a caramel-colored corduroy sport coat with brown leather buttons. Whatever else could be said about him, Thomas surmised, no one could call him a slave to fashion. Smiling, the man held his hand out to Thomas.

"Jerry Fielder," the man said. "You gotta be a Curry, right?"

Thomas shook Fielder's hand a bit uncertainly. "This is Sandy, my wife," Thomas said. "But you undoubtedly knew that already as well."

"Nope," Fielder said, nodding in Sandy's direction. "Glad ta meetcha, Mrs. Curry." He tapped his temple with his index finger. "Logic can only take you so far."

"Well, it's certainly taken you farther than it has me, at least up to this point."

"No big deal," Fielder allowed. "I can see your old man's face all over your puss, and you're sittin' in his seats." This was true. T. Graham Curry had owned the same baseball season tickets to the Polo Grounds since the Hoover administration, and they were the ones Thomas and Sandy were using.

"You know my father?" Thomas asked.

"We had some business with each other back in 'fifty-one, 'fifty-two," Fielder nodded.

Thomas's eyebrows rose slightly. T. Graham Curry, his father and my partner, was a criminal lawyer.

"Well, whatever it was," Thomas said, "I hope it came out all right."

"Hobbs Act rap," Fielder shrugged. "Nineteen months, served ten. Coulda been a lot worse."

"I see. And we owe the special beer run to your appreciation of his efforts?"

"Not exactly." Fielder smiled a trifle sheepishly. "Fact is, there was somethin' I wanted to make sure I didn't miss."

"To wit?"

"To wit," Fielder said, "it's seven to two Throneberry's gonna pop up, and when he does I wanna be sure I hear you explain the infield fly rule to Mrs. Curry here."

The crack of bat on ball jerked their attention abruptly back to the field. Throneberry had just popped up. Two umpires were holding their right arms straight up in the air. The opposing first baseman strolled onto the infield grass. The Mets runners returned to their bases. Throneberry pounded his bat on the ground in frustration. The crowd groaned with disappointment. The first baseman caught the ball.

"Infield fly?" Sandy asked.

"Why don't you explain it?" Thomas demanded, grinning wickedly at Fielder. "Since you brought it up."

"Oookaayyy," Fielder said. "Infield fly rule. Let's see." This hesitation was feigned, for Fielder's voice immediately took on the rattling monotone of rote recitation. "When there're runners on first an' second or the bases are loaded with less'n two out, an' the batter hits a fair fly ball which in the judgment of the umpire could be caught by an infielder playing in his normal position, the umpire shall declare the batter out and the runners may advance at their own risk."

"So the batter who just hit is out?" It was Sandy's question.

10

"Yes."

"He is out because the other side caught the ball he hit?"

"Uh-uh," Fielder said emphatically, shaking his head. "That's the point of the rule, ya see. He was out because he hit a fair ball that an infielder *could* catch. Even if the first baseman had dropped the ball or hadn't even tried for it and let it fall, Throneberry would've been out."

"And why is that?" Sandy asked.

" 'Cause that's what the rule says."

"I mean, why is that the rule?"

" 'Cause otherwise the fielder could deliberately let the ball drop, see, an' get a double play. The pop-up freezes the runners, so if there's no infield fly rule an' the fielders let the ball drop they force alla runners out at their next bases."

"But that would be clever play, no?"

"Well, yeah, I 'spose it would."

"Then why is it against the rules?"

"Ah, well, I guess it would be, ah—" Fielder glanced at Thomas.

"You got yourself into it," Thomas said, "you get yourself out of it."

R.J., the kid who had gone after the beers, reappeared. Fielder seized with relieved delight on the distraction.

"Saved by the beer," Fielder said enthusiastically. "C'mon, everyone, belly up."

The tall young man handed Thomas and Sandy paper cups overflowing with white foam. Thomas took a second look at the kid's hands—large, powerful, meaty, with something about them suggesting that they were somehow graceful as well.

"Thank you," Thomas said.

"R. J., this is Mr. and Mrs. Curry. Mr. and Mrs. Curry, Richard Madden, Boston College, 1960."

"Sandy," Sandy said, extending her hand.

"Rainbow J," Thomas said.

"Please?" Sandy said, perplexed. "Thomas, why should he call you Rainbow Jay? Is that some type of baseball slang?"

"Basketball," Thomas said. "It's not what he should call me, it's what I should call him. Sandy, we're being introduced to one of the best outside shooters to play college basketball on the East Coast in the last five years. Mr. Madden's nickname when he started for Boston College was Rainbow J, because his jump shot looked like a rainbow and it was as good as gold."

"You just made the kid's night," Fielder said to Thomas.

"That's right," R.J. agreed. "There aren't many who still remember."

"It's only been two years," Thomas said.

"Two years is a long time, for a jock—er, athlete," R.J. stammered, glancing at Sandy.

"I think that one American sport per night is my limit," Sandy commented. "I still do not altogether comprehend infield flies."

"It looks like my limit as well," Thomas said. "Getting you and baseball on speaking terms is going to be more demanding than I expected."

The next Mets batter, Elio Chacon, hit a ground ball to the right side. The second baseman fielded it and threw to the shortstop covering second base. The shortstop caught the ball more or less as he crossed the bag, then threw to first. Fielder scribbled in the scorebook on his lap.

"Excuse me," Sandy said to him as she noticed the action. "What did you just do?"

"I scored the play," Fielder explained. "See?"

He showed her the notation he had made in the box opposite Chacon's name under the column for the fourth inning: DP 4-6-3.

Sandy looked intently at the pageful of symmetrical boxes arrayed in lines and columns, some of them filled in with a variety of cryptic numbers, abbreviations, and other symbols. She studied it for close to a minute.

"Do you mean," she asked then, "that you have written down here a note about what just happened?"

"Sure," Fielder said. "Elio Chacon ends the fourth inning

by hittin' into a double play, second-to-short-to-first. So I write that down for his at-bat in the fourth inning: DP four-six-three."

"DP for double play," Sandy said, mesmerized.

"Right."

"But where do the numbers come from? The number of the fielder who caught the ball was not four but twelve, and he does not play the fourth base but the second."

"Ah," Fielder said. "Twelve's the number of the *player* who caught the ball. The number of the fielding position—second baseman—is four."

"You mean, every position has a number given to it, which is always the same, regardless of what player is assigned to that position?"

"Exactly. Pitcher's one, catcher two, first base three, second base four, third base five, shortstop six, left field seven, center field eight, right field nine."

"But this is marvelous," Sandy murmured. She traced back to the bottom of the first inning. " 'Five-three,' " she read. "The first batter for our team hit the ball to the third base fielder, who threw him out at the first-base position?"

"Right."

"For the second batter, you have a line from the home base to the part of the outfield behind second base, and a line drawn to first base, and 'one b' circled. So that means—what?"

"That the—"

"No," she snapped. "Please do not tell me. That means—what? That the batter hit the ball to the outfield and got a one-base hit."

"A single, right," Fielder said. "And since he's a Met, he stays at first for the rest of the inning. That's why the line doesn't go any farther."

"Ah, yes, I see."

Rapt, Sandy proceeded to explore with Fielder, out by out and hit by hit, the scoring of every grounder, strikeout, fly, error, walk, base hit and run in the game to that point.

"Where can one get this?" she asked, tapping the score-book.

Fielder flipped the spiral-bound booklet closed for a moment so that she could see the burgundy cover.

"C.S. Peterson Scoremaster Scorebook," he said. "You can pick one up in any sporting goods store. But you won't need to till next season 'cause this one's now yours." He handed it to her.

"Thank you very much," Sandy said. "But you need not do this."

"I wanna do it," Fielder answered. "In honor of your initiation into the mysteries of the greatest sport ever conceived by the human mind."

"Do you always get this poetic over baseball?" Thomas asked.

"You spend eight years inna parochial school memorizing every poem ever written by a Catholic in English, you gotta be poetic once inna while," Fielder retorted, grinning.

"Thank you," Sandy repeated. "This is formidable. And now I know I will have a scorebook in time for the game tomorrow night."

"The game tomorrow night?" Thomas asked. "You mean you want to go to the ball game again tomorrow?"

"Emphatically. And the night after, if they are playing. I have never dreamed that a game could be charted and recorded at this level of abstraction. It is like describing a fencing match with a series of equations." (You have to understand that for Sandy, who was both an accomplished fencer and a prototypical product of the French educational system, describing a fencing match with a series of equations would be one of the most intellectually engaging prospects she could think of.) "I must learn how to do this."

Chapter Three

So that was how Thomas and Sandy met Jerry Fielder and Richard Madden, a/k/a Rainbow J. On the surface, it didn't look like an acquaintance destined to go much deeper than a couple of beers and a little banter, or to survive very long after the last out in that night's game.

Thomas at thirty-two had a Princeton education and NYU and Columbia degrees. He also had four million dollars inherited from his mother. He was a lawyer although not an attorney since, as he sometimes testily pointed out, he had voluntarily surrendered his law license in order to disabuse certain people of the impression that they could control him by threatening to take it away.

Sandy spoke three modern languages, devoted at least ten hours a week to a treatise she was writing on geography, and was more likely to spend her free time in an art gallery or a bookstore than a sports stadium. She liked sports that involved her doing something—tennis, fencing, horseback riding—rather than the spectator variety.

You wouldn't have thought either one of them would have much in common with a has-been college hoops star, much less someone who'd served time for interfering with interstate commerce by extortion—which is what you have to do to violate the Hobbs Act—and who, as Thomas noticed, went to baseball games carrying a handgun in a shoulder holster underneath the left armpit of his corduroy jacket.

But there was more to Thomas and Sandy than met the eye. Superficial judgments about them usually turned out to be wrong.

Several years before, for example, Thomas had fled what was then French Algeria one step ahead of the guillotine, in the process saving Sandy and her mother and sister from a nationalist massacre. The nationalists had killed Sandy's father, an officer who'd stayed at his post—and in June, 1962, Sandy had married the man who'd spent several months flying guns to those same nationalists. Anyone who shrugged Thomas off as an Eastside fop or took Sandy for a soft, charming Parisienne misread the situation. Thomas's silk-stocking/stagedoor-johnny routine was ninety percent pose, a shield he held up to keep the world from knowing what was going on behind his eyebrows. And Sandy was neither soft nor Parisian, and was charming only when she chose to be, which was by no means all of the time.

As we all found out later, Fielder wasn't likely to make superficial judgments about people like Thomas and Sandy or anyone else. In reflecting on it over the years, though, I've come to believe that there was something more behind the quick, sympathetic acquaintance that sprang up between him and them. Thomas and Sandy were passionately in love with each other—though they weren't exactly the billing and cooing type, as I expect you've noticed—but there was a different kind of affection between them as well. They weren't only lovers, they were friends, the way men can be who have nothing sexual between them but who have shared intense and defining experiences. I think Fielder sensed that and it appealed to him.

Of course, he also had an ulterior motive. But they didn't find out about that until it was too late.

Anyway, Fielder and R.J. and Thomas and Sandy ended up spending quite a bit of time together over the next few weeks. After the game where they met, they adjourned to the Peg, a saloon near the Polo Grounds that Fielder knew about, and talked until closing time. They talked about baseball, the Hobbs Act, unions, the United States Army, religion, politics, and philosophy, on all of which Fielder had decided opinions.

On religion, for example, Fielder professed delight when he learned that Sandy still went to mass.

"I thought the only practicing Catholics left in America were micks an' people in Bing Crosby movies," he said, shaking his head.

" 'Micks'?" asked Sandy, whose impressive command of American English didn't extend to some of our more colorful ethnic epithets.

"Irish," Thomas explained.

"In that case," Sandy said to Fielder, "there is at least one practicing Catholic in America who fits into neither category."

"I'm a bit fallen away myself," Fielder said. "They still have guardian angels, don't they?"

"Naturally," Sandy smiled.

"You know what one of my kids asks me a few weeks ago? It's my five-year-old, Sean. He asks me do guardian angels have names, or can each of us give our own guardian angel whatever name we want to."

"What did you tell him?" This question came from Thomas, who was not a Catholic, practicing, fallen away, or of any other variety.

"I said they got names, a course. Like mine, for an example, is named Fast Eddie. But sometimes he lets me call him by his nickname, Slick."

For blasphemy not much more egregious than that, a troop of Sandy's ancestors had worked the Albigensians over quite thoroughly, and I mean *quite* thoroughly—when was the last time you saw an Albigensian? Sandy, however, reacted by laughing convulsively and spritzing Budweiser into the smoky haze floating over the table.

Thomas and Sandy saw Fielder and R.J. together several more times before September 26. Sometimes there were others along, although never the wife, Mary Margaret, or the four children that Fielder claimed. Usually they met at ball games or at the Peg afterward. Once before an afternoon game they had an impromptu sandwich-and-coffee snack at the Columbus Avenue Gym, which was on Forty-second Street rather than anywhere near Columbus Avenue and where Fielder seemed to have an office and a number of acquaintances with more muscles than teeth. It was on this occasion that Fielder introduced Sandy to corned beef, which met with her unqualified approval.

Thinking back on this series of ostensibly happenstantial get-togethers, Thomas and Sandy couldn't remember a single thing R.J. had said at any of them. Almost at will, though, they could quote Fielder on, say, the Army and the Hobbs Act:

"I turn eighteen too late to fight in the big one. Guess I can thank Fast Eddie for that. My birthday's two days before the Krauts surrender. So I figure they'll send me to fight the Japs but Hiroshima takes care a that 'fore I'm through basic. Fast Eddie again. But Uncle Sam still has this perfec'ly good red-haired mick who's learned close-order drill an' everythin' an' they don't want that to go to waste so they send me to Germany after all. Occupation Forces. That was some occupation, lemme tell ya. I get there, it's *alles kaput in Deutschland.* That's what everyone calls it. Time I left, they're callin' it 'the German economic miracle.' An' lemme tell ya somethin'. In between *alles kaput in Deutschland* an' the German economic miracle, some guys who knew what they were doin' got plenty rich."

18

"How about you?" Thomas asked at that point.

"Nah, not me," Fielder laughed. "I was this eighteen-year-old kid from Hell's Kitchen whose dad was a labor organizer, I did what they told me. My reward is, I get back here an' I get to go to night school on the G.I. Bill. Studied business administration, concentration in finance."

"Interesting major for someone whose father was a labor organizer."

"Lemme tell ya, ya wouldn't believe it but it's Dad's idea. I get back he says to me, 'Jer, brass knuckles and lead pipes ain' gonna do it anymore. It's past that now. Lotta these boys 're fat an' happy, we're gonna need guys who can read the fine print on financial statements as much as we need the rough an' ready types.' So I study balance sheets an' double-entry accounting an' I end up in the tank on a Hobbs Act rap." He laughed bitingly at the memory. "Can ya beat that?"

"You must've been doing something for extra credit," Thomas said.

"Ya know what, that's exactly what it was. Exactly. In a way."

"Exactly in a way?"

"Ya know what I mean."

"I'm not alto—"

"Okay, so lemme tell ya. Organizer comes up to me—it wasn' Dad, he was dead by then—anyway, this organizer comes up to me an' says the truck farmers are bringin' their own produce in from Jersey, am I in? This is in 'fifty-one. Now, ordinarily, I'd a hadda few questions. But I'm three-fourths a the way through this night school course an' I'm talkin' to this guy's spent half his life on picket lines an' plant-gate brawls an' I didn' fight in the big one, an' I figure I got somethin' to prove. Extra credit, like you said. So I say sure, count me in."

"In on what?"

"Well, there's this street, see, about two miles from the Farmers' Market in Brooklyn where it gets real narrow an' there's no way they can maneuver even a pickup truck. So

19

some buddies an' me are waitin' about four in the mornin' an' the first truck comes by, we jump up on the running board when the driver has to slow down. I show 'im a tire iron an' he kills the engine real fast an' gets out. I ask 'im has he gotta union card an' a course he don't. So I say, buddy, you owe Local twenty-three fourteen dollars 'n twenty-eight cents—that's eight hours' pay for a union driver, see—pay up. He says stick it, so we turn his truck over an' use about two gallons a high-test to quick-fry his rabbit food for 'im."

"You did ten months for that?"

"Ten months an' change. Valentine's to Christmas Eve, 1952. I know whatcha mean. It seems like a lot. Far as I'm concerned, we're just enforcin' a union shop contract, that's all. But your dad said I coulda gotta lot more."

"Well," Sandy said, "at least you proved something, no?"

"Ya bet I proved somethin', Mrs. Curry. I proved I was one dumb mick, that's what I proved. Ain' that right, R.J.?"

R.J. laughed and continued his assault on the second half of a boilermaker.

"I get out an' ya know what I get? Ten months at sixty-one-twenty a week."

"They gave you a job?" Thomas asked.

"Ya could call it that."

"Doing what?"

"Showin' up on Fridays to pick up my check."

"Ah. Sort of a symmetrical reward then. Ten months of soft labor in exchange for ten months of hard labor."

"Yeh. Sorta. 'Cept this organizer who set the whole thing up, while I'm on the inside makin' little ones outta big ones he gets elected business manager of Teamsters Local twenty-three. When he comes by to tell me about ten months at sixty-one-twenty a week, he's drivin' a Buick. It was Germany all over again."

"I'm not sure I follow you."

"I mean, some guys make out an' some guys do what they're told. I mean, I thought it over an' I said to myself, 'Jerry Fielder ain' been goin' about things the right way."

"That's when you decided to open the gym?"

"That's a good one, that is," Fielder laughed. "No, that's when I decided maybe I should try doin' things a little different. Ya know what the great thing about America is?"

"Somehow I'm sure you're going to tell me."

"The great thing about this country is, everybody gets his very own way to beat the system. Micks, wops, Jews, colored fellas, we all get our own hustle. It's just a question a findin' your way. Guts an' keepin' your eyes open's all it takes."

"A toast," Thomas said at that point, clinking his beer glass with Sandy's, "to the American dream."

And everybody laughed.

Chapter Four

There are certain moments in every well-lived life that you look back on as perfect. They're not necessarily the most important or the times of greatest happiness. They're just intervals of contentment that couldn't have been improved on. Changing any detail, altering any nuance of the event would have diminished it. You try to remember it exactly the way it was, because that was exactly the way it should have been.

Thomas and Sandy looked back on the Columbus Avenue Gym lunch on September 22 as one of those moments. They ate gathered around the scarred, wooden desk in Fielder's basement office, the air heavy with the pungent odor of Absorbine, Jr. and Atomic Balm, their conversation accompanied by the rhythmic thud of fists pummeling body bags a few feet outside the door and the skidding, high-pitched squeak of basketball shoes on hardwood on the floor above them.

If Thomas or Sandy was ever able to isolate what was so special about eating delicatessen sandwiches and drinking mediocre coffee in this plebian ambience, they didn't share it with me. It was the prelude to a crisp, autumn afternoon spent watching baseball being played in the sunshine where God intended for it to be played. It was an hour of comfortable talk among people who found each other intriguing. Maybe that was it. Then again, maybe it was the confrontation at the game afterward.

There weren't any trophies in Fielder's office, no mementos of seasons past, no curling photographs of boxers or ballplayers looking out of memory-gilded yesterdays into a present that could never measure up. The office was a place to do the not clearly specified business that Fielder did, not a shrine to bygone athletic ages. It featured a four-drawer filing cabinet, securely locked, and a brace of folding chairs. On the desk, an enormous, old-fashioned, black, rounded-end adding machine—the kind with one hundred keys and a crank— dwarfed the no-nonsense, black, rotary-dial telephone next to it. There had been four magazines on the desk when Thomas and Sandy came in—*Sports Illustrated, The New Yorker, Saturday Evening Post,* and *Ring*—but R.J. had scooped these over to a smaller table nearby that seemed to serve as his personal domain.

The office was anything but tidy, Sandy noticed as Fielder set out on the desk the corned beef sandwiches and napkins that R.J. had fetched, but there was nothing careless about the disarray. There were no letters or papers or adding machine tapes lying around. Whatever Fielder did in the office, he didn't display it casually to acquaintances he'd invited there because it was a convenient place to have lunch before an afternoon baseball game.

They spent most of this lunch talking about politics: How President Kennedy had made the steel companies back down from an announced price increase, the space race that *Life* magazine thought the Russians would win in 1965, Governor Rockefeller's low opinion of New York City Mayor Robert

Wagner, Fielder's low opinion of a state-run lottery ("It'd be a gratuitous insult to gamblers everywhere to associate their ancient an' honorable profession with the disreputable enterprise of financing government")—in other words, about what most people in New York who discussed politics that day talked about. Toward the end of the meal, though, Fielder asked Thomas two questions that five days or so later began to look portentous.

"You're supposed to know somethin' about law, right?"

"Columbia Law School thought so a few years ago anyway."

"Okay. Lemme run one by ya. Guy tells me a while back, if I pull a fast one on someone but he like *knows* it's a fast one, that ain't fraud. Is that on the level?"

"Sure," Thomas said after only a moment's reflection. "The victim has to reasonably rely on the fraudulent statement. That's an element of any claim for fraud. So if your intended victim knows you're putting one over on him, there's no fraud. Of course, there's also probably no fast one."

"Thanks. I was wonderin' about that."

"Anytime. Anything specific you'd like to discuss?"

"Sure. First game a the Series. Looks like Whitey Ford against Juan Marichal, right, the way the Dodgers're chokin'? Who d'ya like?"

"You know," Thomas said, "I occasionally do free-lance legal work for my father's partner, Theodore Furst. He once had me check on the penalty for violating an FTC consent decree. I asked if one of his clients was thinking of violating one—and he answered me about the same way you did just now."

"I gotta like Ford myself," Fielder said. "Whadda you think, Mrs. Curry?"

"I think that if someone has answered a question, there is no point in asking it again."

"I like that." Fielder glanced at his watch. "Hey, we better get goin'. We got less'n a half hour."

That was when Fielder asked his second oblique-angle question.

"Hey, what're you two doin' on the twenty-sixth? Tell ya' what, I got somethin' special goin' at the game that night."

"Perhaps we should discuss it while making progress toward the game this afternoon."

"We're goin', we're goin'," Fielder said. "Take it easy, big guy. I mean it about the twenty-sixth though. I'm bringin' Mary Margaret, which the two a you hasn't met yet, an' some other folks, and here's the best part: We're in the press box."

"How did you manage that?"

"Well, I don't know if you've noticed, but this lovable buffoon act the Amazin' Mets've been puttin' on has started wearin' a bit thin now that it's September an' there's a little nip in the air. I told 'em I could produce ten or more warm bodies for a late-season game, an' I talked 'em into it. I really want you an' Mrs. Curry should come."

Thomas glanced questioningly at Sandy.

"It is a night game?" Sandy asked.

"Yep."

"Count on us."

Fielder reasonably relied on this statement. To his detriment.

Chapter
Five

Dick Groat, thrown uncharacteristically off stride by a Roger Craig curveball, stroked a handle hit toward the hole at short. Felix Mantilla, the Mets' third baseman, cut in front of the shortstop, fielded the ball cleanly, and threw to second to force out Bill Mazeroski. The second baseman threw on to first, but the Mets' double play combinations were unequal even to a leadfoot like Groat and he was safe.

FC 5-4, Sandy wrote in her scorebook opposite Groat's name in the column for the first inning. Fielder's choice, third to second. Then she drew a line from home plate to first to show that Groat himself had reached base safely.

It was September 22, 1962. The Mets were playing the Pittsburgh Pirates. Sandy had the C.S. Peterson Scoremaster Scorebook that Fielder had given her and her own copy of the Official Baseball Rules, with which she had by now become thoroughly familiar. She didn't do things by halves.

"Bums," someone muttered two rows down, by way of commentary on the failed double play effort. "It's enough to make ya a Yankee fan."

"Can ya believe that guy?" Fielder asked Thomas, gesturing with his pencil toward the mutterer.

"No," Thomas said, after considering the question carefully. "The Mets are terrible, but they'd have to be a lot worse before I'd consider watching baseball with stockbrokers and advertising copywriters whose concept of offensive strategy is to wait for someone to hit a three-run homer."

"Listen," a young man in the mutterer's row said emphatically, turning around and pointing a finger aggressively at Thomas, "don't knock da Yanks. Don't knock da Bronx Bombers." He pronounced this "bronce bommuhs." "At least dey didn' leave town."

"No," Thomas said, "they just drove out the teams that did."

"Dat's bull!" the young man yelped. His neck stiffened inside the collar of his black leather jacket. "Listen—"

"Knock it off, Tony," an older man sitting three seats away from the Yankees partisan said. Tony instantly shut up. Thomas would have guessed that the man who produced this effect was forty-five or a little older. His hair was very short and consisted of interspersed white and charcoal-gray bristles. He turned his head slightly. "Fancy company you're keepin', Jerry-boy," he said to Fielder.

"This is Thomas Andrew Curry and Sandy, his wife," Fielder said. "They know their baseball. Mr. an' Mrs. Curry, that's Harry Liebniewicz, International Brotherhood of Teamsters, Chauffeurs, Warehousemen and Helpers." Fielder pronounced the name correctly, Leeb-NAY-vich. "He's a good guy, 'cept he seems to of got stuck baby-sittin' a buncha j.d.'s he ain't had time to send to charm school yet."

Liebniewicz laughed drily. "Solidarity forever," he said.

"Yeah. Speakin' a that, I got somethin' I wanna talk to you about, you get a chance later on."

"That's what I heard," Liebniewicz said. "That's wunna the reasons I'm here."

"What about the kiddie corps?"

"See me in the head around the fourth inning."

Liebniewicz turned his face front and center. Tony and two colleagues, who had just been dismissed as juvenile delinquents in a conversation that went over all of their heads, did the same. Fielder relaxed and settled back in his seat.

"Hey," he said to Thomas. "You never got around to tellin' me who you want in the first game of the Series."

"I want the Giants. Naturally."

"How much?"

"With all my heart. But sentiment has nothing to do with wagering, if that's what you're asking."

"That's what I'm askin'. I already told ya I gotta like Ford myself. Someday soon the Yanks are all gonna wake up old the same morning: Mantle, Maris, Kubek, Richardson, Boyer, Skowron, Berra, Howard, Ford. All of 'em. An' then people are gonna wonder what was so great about the almighty Yankees. But this year ain't the year."

"An' not next year or a whole lotta years after that," Tony said sullenly, without turning around but loudly enough for Fielder to hear.

"Two more years, Tony," Fielder called down. "I give 'em two more years, tops."

"What do you think about it, Sandy?" Thomas asked.

Sandy finished totaling the hits and runs at the bottom of the first column before she looked up to answer the question.

"It is formidable. In five minutes of talking about a game this group has managed to exemplify both fallacies that define twentieth century thought: the confusion of passion with truth, and the use of aesthetic criteria to make moral judgments."

"You hear that, Tony?" Fielder called. "We *really* messed up."

"Don't take it too seriously," Thomas said. "You'll only encourage her."

Relative peace reigned until the bottom of the second inning, when Mets pitcher Al Jackson succeeded in striking out Bill Virdon, the Pirates' center fielder. Unfortunately for the Mets, their catcher didn't succeed in catching the third strike, which squirted away from him and rolled toward the third-base dugout. Virdon raced safely to first.

"That is scored K-slash-E-two, correct?" Sandy asked.

Thomas blinked and tried to remember the arcane scoring formula for the unusual play that had just occurred.

"That's right," Fielder said instantly. "K for strikeout, with the batter going to first on an error charged to the catcher. You knew that, didn' ya, Tony?"

"Shaddap," Tony muttered.

"Course Tony knew that," Fielder said placidly to Thomas and Sandy. "That's one a the five ways for a batter to reach first without the bat touchin' the ball, right, Tony?"

"They're only four ways, smart guy," Tony said, provoked once again to the point of swiveling around in his seat.

"Five, Tony." Fielder held up his right hand, palm out and open. "Like the amendment you plead in front of grand juries. If you haven' come up with all five by the end of the game, maybe Mrs. Curry here'll tell ya the one ya don' know."

Tony resisted this impish tease for almost fifteen seconds. Then you could tell, just by looking at the back of his head, that he'd started puzzling over it. By the bottom of the third inning, he was surreptitiously analyzing the problem with the colleague seated next to him.

With one out in the top of the fourth, Fielder, R.J., and Liebniewicz adjourned discreetly to the nearest men's room for the discussion Fielder had alluded to in the first inning. When the top of the inning was over, Thomas stood up, declared his intention to find another beer, and asked Sandy if she wanted one. Concentrating on her scorebook, she held up her nearly full cup and shook her head.

Tony and his friend were still struggling with Fielder's intellectual puzzle.

"All right, let's see," Tony said quietly. "Walk." He held out one finger. "Hit by pitch." He punched out a second finger. "That's two."

"Passed ball on a third strike, like we saw last inning," the colleague reminded him.

"Oh, right. That's three."

"And then catcher's interference."

"What's that?" Tony demanded uncertainly.

"Like if the batter swings and hits the catcher's mitt 'cause the catcher's leaning too far over the plate." The colleague's tone suggested that this esoteric rule was common knowledge in the community of educated men and women.

"Sure, that's right," Tony agreed, as if he knew the rule as well as he knew his mother's birthday. "Catcher's interference. That's four. Now what's five?"

"Yeah, what's five?"

"There isn't five," Tony said decisively. "There's only four, like I said. He was just yankin' our chain. Ain't that right, mam'selle?" he called over his shoulder.

Sandy glanced up in mild exasperation, then went back to her scorebook without responding to the maladroit question.

"I mean, you agree, doncha, mam'selle? Only four ways, right?"

"No," Sandy said then. "You are forgetting the catcher's balk."

"What?" Tony demanded.

"Catcher's balk," she repeated. "Rule seven-point-oh-seven. If a runner is trying to score from third base on a squeeze or a steal and the catcher steps on or in front of home plate without possession of the ball, a balk is called on the pitcher, the ball is dead, and the batter is awarded first base."

Tony chose to find a nuance of mockery in Sandy's straightforward answer. The fact that the other Teamsters in Tony's row found her explanation side-splitting didn't help.

"Sure, catcher's balk," one of them yelled at Tony. "Everyone knows about that, right?" They guffawed.

Tony stood up. A stride brought him to within a yard of Sandy, who continued to ignore him.

"Rule seven-point-oh-seven, huh?" he asked.

"Yes," Sandy answered.

"Yeah. I thought dat was what you said."

"You tell 'er, Tony," came derisively from the Teamster row, along with more laughter.

"Now you tell her a rule, Tony," another of his colleagues suggested, to further merriment.

Sandy glanced up. She assumed now, incorrectly, that the other Teamsters were directing their ridicule at her rather than Tony. This irritated her. The glint in those royal blue eyes I mentioned was suddenly hard and chilly against the background of her smooth, brown, Latin face.

"It is a very well-known rule," she said. "Outside this section."

Tony wasn't a model of self-control under the best of circumstances. Sandy's gibe pushed him over the edge. He turned toward his colleagues and smiled.

"She's gotta lip, that one has," he said. Then, deliberately and in as offensive a way as he could, Tony poured Irish coffee onto her scorebook.

"She has an arm too," Sandy spat, and dashed the beer in her cup into Tony's face.

Thomas saw this gesture from the top of the ramp. It was the first inkling he had that something dramatic might be developing. He dropped the beer he was carrying and ran toward the scene. The remaining Teamsters converged on it from the opposite direction. Fielder and R. J. reached the top of the ramp a moment after Thomas had left it. They dashed without hesitation toward the impending melee.

The fight, if it had happened, might have been interesting. Tony tried to backhand Sandy, but she was used to ducking fencing foils that moved a lot faster than his hand did. He succeeded only in bruising his knuckles on the back of the seat in front of where Sandy would have been if she hadn't darted out of the way.

Taking advantage of Tony's momentary loss of balance, Sandy boxed his right ear, in exactly the way that a parent might have slapped a misbehaving child back when that sort of thing was still done to misbehaving children.

Things stopped there because Liebniewicz arrived and quickly took charge.

"Please don't hit him again," Liebniewicz called calmly. "I've got first dibs."

An off-duty cop picking up extra money as a stadium security guard was moving toward the scene.

"We're heading out," Liebniewicz said, forestalling any inquiries. He clapped Fielder on the shoulder with the back of his hand. "Be in touch."

"Right."

Then he held out his hand to Thomas, who shook it.

"Hell of a girl you've got there," he said.

September 26

U.S. IS PREPARED TO SEND TROOPS AS
MISSISSIPPI GOVERNOR DEFIES
COURT AND BARS NEGRO STUDENT
   New York Times, Sept. 26,
   1962, p. 1, cols. 4–8

SOVIET TRAWLERS TO USE NEW PORT
PLANNED IN CUBA
   New York Times, Sept. 26,
   1962, p. 1, col. 3

GOVERNOR ROCKEFELLER CHARGED
YESTERDAY THAT NEW YORK CITY
WAS "ONE OF THE WORST GOVERNED
CITIES IN THE ENTIRE NATION."
   New York Times, Sept. 26,
   1962, p. 1, col. 6

U.S. PLANE PERILED IN LANE TO
BERLIN—RUSSIAN FIGHTERS HARASS
IT AND A FRENCH AIRLINER
   New York Times, Sept. 26,
   1962, p. 3, col. 5

The way of the champion was an old story . . . to the
New York Yankees, who downed the Washington Sen-
ators, 8 to 3, to clinch their 27th American League pennant and their third in a row.
   New York Times, Sept. 26, 1962, p. 41, col. 3

Chapter Six

"T erm loan agreement, original and three?"

"Yes."

"Financing statement?"

"Yes, two duplicate original counterparts and three copies."

"Promissory note of Schellenwerk, GmbH?

"Yes."

And so on through all the documentation of a seven-figure, international, dollar-denominated commercial transaction: the board of directors resolutions; the personal guaranty of Joachim Schellen; the subordination agreement executed by Kommerzbank, Frankfurt-am-Main; the written opinion of German counsel; the written opinion of British counsel; and, last but far from trivial, the written opinion of New York counsel.

Namely, me.

The transaction described is in all respects lawful under the applicable laws of the United States and of the State of New York, and the several agreements, notes, drafts, and instruments are cognizable under such laws, fully effective and enforceable according to their terms. Signed: Curry & Furst by Theodore Furst, member of the firm.

Bracing when you think about it. David Rockefeller's bank and the large and powerful law firm representing it were insisting on an opinion-of-counsel from Curry & Furst, with its two partners and six associates and distinctly human-scale practice. Which meant that if Curry & Furst was wrong, five minor Fursts from two marriages who were planning on Yale and Mount Holyoke would be working their way through CCNY instead.

This had all come about because I'd taken the trouble to learn about something called Eurodollars back when not many people knew about them. Eurodollars were the collateral securing the loan that Chase Manhattan was making to a German client of mine called Schellenwerk, GmbH.

Eurodollars aren't dollars. Dollars are pieces of green paper issued by the United States government. In 1962, there were still some dollars around called silver certificates, and you could take one of those to the Sub-Treasury in New York City and get a little plastic Baggie of silver dust for it.

Eurodollars are data entries: rectangular holes cut into computer cards and magnetic blips on tape reels in Bordeaux or Milan or Geneva or Manchester. A very bright European named Siegmund Warburg was willing to bet that you could translate those data entries into brick and mortar, concrete, highways, and factories. I was willing to bet that he was right.

That was why Sandy and I were in my office at 9:00 A.M., bright and early by New York standards, on September 26, 1962, going through the tedious chore of preparing documents for the closing of Chase Manhattan's loan to Schellenwerk. The closing was scheduled to start at 11:00 A.M. the following day.

For around nine months I'd devoted at least half my working time to putting this transaction together. If it closed, one of the first payments made from the loan proceeds would be a check for $83,000, made out to Curry & Furst and representing about one-third of the firm's total 1962 revenue. If the loan didn't close, Curry & Furst was going to write off five months of its junior partner's billable time for the year.

I had hired Sandy a little over two years before. She'd recently resigned from a clerical position with the French U.N. mission. She'd resigned in order to avoid betraying her country or dishonoring herself, and she'd left rather precipitately. As a consequence she'd had what I needed in a Girl Friday: European language skills; intelligence; initiative; and a desperate need for a job, resulting in a congenial willingness to work cheap.

Now she had a husband whose after-tax income need never fall below $80,000 a year, which in 1962 was ample to support a very comfortable life in New York City. She no longer had to get up in the morning and work for the relative pittance I could afford to pay her. I never asked her why she continued to do so, but I think if I had she would have said it was because she was indispensable and irreplaceable. She would have been right.

Sandy was pert rather than beautiful, her intelligence was lancing and analytic rather than creative, and she could be impatient with people who weren't as quick as she was. But in any spot from a loan closing to a knife fight in a dark alley, she'd be one of the people I'd ask to have on my side.

While Sandy and I were putting the closing file together, Thomas was using his time more agreeably. He was at Calliphonics Ltd., a discreet, exclusive hi-fi equipment shop on Park Avenue.

For a male under thirty-five in 1962, this was a ritualized

and immensely solemn undertaking. Back then you could read more tips in *Playboy* magazine about how to get the right hi-fi outfit than you could about how to seduce desirable women or end encumbering affairs. A man who might spend forty-five minutes shopping for a suit and devote no more than a morning and part of an afternoon to selecting and buying a car could turn the purchase of a stereo into a three-month project, talking to learned aficionados, reviewing the annual stereo issue of *Esquire*, and drawing up matrices of features and prices.

Thomas had traversed these stages and reached the point where he actually felt prepared to go into a shop and choose some hardware. For seventy-three minutes, Thomas had been sitting in a comfortably padded leather chair in a sound-proofed room, sipping from a crystal tumbler of orange juice over shaved ice, and listening to test albums and tapes playing over a collection of Blaupak amplifiers, Dinesen turntables, Bose speakers, and Roberts 990 reel-to-reel tape decks. Calliphonics was one of a very small number of authorized retail distributors officially allowed to sell these highly reputed German and American products in the New York area. (Back then, the closest the Japanese came to sophisticated consumer electronics was transistor radios.)

This kind of lavish attention was standard procedure at Calliphonics for any customer who looked like he might be persuaded to spend as much as a thousand dollars on the store's products. With the healthy markups that the limited number of authorized retail distributors allowed, spending a thousand dollars wasn't hard, even at 1962 prices.

"Hey, TAC, what're you doin' here?"

Thomas and the salesman, who'd just come out of the demonstration room, looked at once in the direction of Jerry Fielder's raucous voice. Fielder, dressed in his usual blue jeans and corduroy sport coat outfit, stood beside a short, bespectacled man in a charcoal gray, three-piece suit. They were standing outside a walnut door with "H. Feldman, Proprietor" lettered on it in dignified gold capitals.

Thomas walked over, shook hands with Fielder, and was introduced to Harvey Feldman, founder and owner of Calliphonics Ltd. The salesman, exuding self-assurance only a moment before, passed the time bowing and scraping.

"I'm looking for something to spend some money on," Thomas said when he got around to answering Fielder's question.

"We'll see ya at the game tonight, right?"

"You couldn't keep us away. Especially Sandy."

"That's great. I'll have R.J. drop by your dad's shop this afternoon with the tix an' the press-box pass."

"That should work fine. I think Sandy wants to leave work between four-fifteen and four-thirty so that we'll have plenty of time to change and have dinner before the game."

"R.J.'ll have everything there by three at the latest." Fielder pivoted and tapped Harvey Feldman on the chest with a roll of gray and yellow printed, hole-punched papers. "An' hey, Harv, you treat this guy right, okay? No HK business with him, okay? Otherwise, I'll tell 'im about B. Weldon Corbett."

Without waiting for a response to this instruction, Fielder carried his nervous, infectious, Herald Square energy out of the sepulchral dignity of Calliphonics and onto Park Avenue.

"Good Lord," the salesman said.

"I suppose you could say that," Feldman said.

"I wonder who B. Weldon Corbett is," Thomas said.

The salesman shuffled and studied the toes of his loafers. Feldman removed his black, horn-rimmed glasses, took out a white handkerchief, and began sedulously polishing the lenses.

"B. Weldon Corbett," he said quietly and quite calmly, "is a malignant pond scum, metastasizing at a terrifying rate across the surface of New York retailing."

*   *   *

By noon, Sandy and I had done everything possible to get ready for tomorrow's closing. All the arrangements were made, the conference rooms reserved, the cable time cleared, the wire transfers in place, the documents collated, tabbed, and indexed. I told Sandy that I didn't see any reason for her not to meet Thomas for lunch.

I decided to lunch at my club. In the lobby of our building, I snapped a quarter solidly—they were 100 percent silver back then—on the counter of the news-and-tobacco vendor and asked for that morning's *Times*. Francis Xavier Corcoran picked my quarter up, felt with both hands around the paper he was giving me to make sure it was a *Times* and not a *Daily News* or a *Herald Tribune*, and slipped me my change, all in less time than it would have taken most people who could see.

"Have a good lunch, Mr. Furst," he said.

"Thanks, Fran. I'll see you this afternoon."

"That's easy for you to say."

He smiled and I laughed. I knew he couldn't hear a smile.

I went out onto the street, found a cab, and gave the driver the address of the Bachelors' Club. The B-Club was an unpretentious mid-town private association open to any lawfully married male over twenty-nine years of age, holding a college degree, and able to afford its exorbitant dues. On the first floor, members were allowed to entertain any guests they chose as long as they were male. On the second floor, members were allowed to entertain any guests they chose as long as they were female and not married to a member. (The suggestion of spicy naughtiness that this implies was largely spurious. Most members used the club's upstairs bedrooms as I did: for solitary slumber on nights when business kept me in the city.)

As the cab jolted toward my destination, I read through that day's lead story. The governor of Mississippi was defying a federal court order requiring his state's university to admit a black man named James Meredith. President Kennedy said he was ready to send the United States Army to Mississippi to enforce the order if he had to. Ninety-seven years after Appomattox, Mississippi wondered if he meant it. I conjured up a mental image of American soldiers in combat fatigues leveling fixed bayonets at American civilians.

My mind drifted for a moment back to Chase Manhattan's impending loan to Schellenwerk, GmbH. One thing about the *Times*: It puts things in perspective.

Chapter Seven

It's important for lawyers to take an active role in civic affairs. Elections, for example. Many elective offices are quite important. New York County Clerk of Courts comes to mind. By taking an interest in such offices, a lawyer can make an important contribution to the democratic process.

In the case of the 1962 election for New York County Clerk of Courts, I had made a three-figure contribution to the incumbent. That was why I got the phone call at 4:45 in the afternoon on September 26. I still get a little gut clinch when I think about it.

A voice I didn't recognize asked me if Curry & Furst hadn't filed a collection action about three years ago for some German outfit called Schellenwerk. I said I vaguely remembered it.

"Well, this is Terry Mokeski over in the New York County Clerk of Courts' office. I work for Mr. Delahanty." Dennis Delahanty being the incumbent, it would follow that Mr.

Mokeski and everyone else in that office worked for him. Mr. Mokeski mentioned the obvious in order to make sure I understood why I was getting this special treatment. I did.

"I see," I told Mokeski. "What can I do for you?"

"I thought you might like to know some character just blew in here all outta breath and filed a lawsuit against Schellenwerk and Chase Manhattan Bank."

Suddenly it was very cold in the pit of my stomach.

"Who's the plaintiff?"

"Spindle Lathe Company."

"What kind of suit is it?"

"Not sure. Thing is, soon as he files it he wants to know what judge it's assigned to. I told him it's Judge Herzog but he might as well keep his shirt on 'cause Judge Herzog is on vacation through the end of the month. Then he wants to know who the duty judge is."

TRO, I thought. Temporary restraining order. An emergency injunction, granted without a hearing.

My throat was dry. My heart was beating faster than it should have been.

"Who is the duty judge?" I asked.

"Judge Sims."

A bead of perspiration ran from my forehead down my right cheek as I asked the next question. I had a vision of the TRO already signed and in the hands of a deputy sheriff.

"Do you have Judge Sims's number?"

"Save your dime. Judge Sims isn't in. The duty judge went off duty a little early today."

Mokeski chuckled. I made an inarticulate sound.

"I talked to his clerk, though," Mokeski continued. "He penciled this guy in for an emergency hearing at eight tomorrow morning."

"Without notice to the other side?"

"He'll say Chase Manhattan was closed when he got there with the papers, and your client's in Germany, isn't it?"

"All right," I said. "Thank you for letting me know about this. Now I need to ask a favor." I glanced at my watch. It was 4:47. "Can I get someone over right away to read whatever's been filed and get an idea of what the lawsuit's about?"

"I can't go too late but if you get him over here by five-twenty or so I'll hold the door open for him."

"Thank you very much, Mr. Mokeski. I appreciate it."

I'd like the record to show that I didn't panic at this point. For about twenty-five minutes, in fact, I put on an admirable display of what might have passed for grace under pressure. Few things concentrate the faculties so wonderfully as raw fear combined with incipient rage.

Almost before the phone was back in its cradle I was out in the hall bawling the name of Ron Collins, the youngest associate I could think of. I sent him off to Mr. Mokeski's precincts to read the pleadings and report back to me about them. Before Collins had reached the elevator I was calling in more sedate but still urgent tones to Mrs. Walbach at her citadel.

"Yes, Mr. Furst?" Her purse already on her desk, her typewriter already covered, she glanced around at me accusingly.

"An emergency has come up. Would you please ask one of the secretaries if she wouldn't mind working late tonight?"

"None of the girls will be able to stay on notice this short, Mr. Furst." My face paled at this implacable and unappealable judgment. Then she took the cover off of her typewriter. "I'll stay myself."

"Thank you very much."

I went back to my office. It was just about midnight in Frankfurt. I wasn't looking forward to calling Herr Schellen and telling him that there might be a snag, but that was the next thing I had to do.

This call lasted twenty minutes. I began by explaining what little I knew of what had happened.

At first Herr Schellen couldn't understand. Such a thing couldn't happen in Germany. *Ja*, Herr Schellen, but this happens to be the United States. Then he was indignant. This was an outrage. *Ja*, Herr Schellen, but the priority at the moment is to keep it from derailing the loan. Then he was evasive. Spindle Lathe Company, Herr Schellen? Never heard of it. Never? Well, perhaps many years ago Schellenwerk might have guaranteed a debt owed to some company with a name something like that by a U.S. company involved in a joint venture with Schellenwerk. But that was all over and done with.

"You mean the debt was paid and the guaranty discharged?"

Well, no, not paid, exactly. Refinanced.

"All right. But the guaranty was discharged?"

Well, no, not discharged exactly. It was just that after the refinancing everyone recognized that the loan no longer had anything to do with Schellenwerk. The guaranty was obsolete. Ancient history.

"But not discharged?"

No. Not exactly. But all the collateral securing the debt originally was released.

I saw a tiny pinpoint of light on the farthest horizon defined by the black clouds that otherwise filled the sky.

"You mean the collateral the debtor put up in the first place was released when the loan was refinanced?"

"*Ja*, Herr Furst."

"Without your consent?"

"*Ja*, of course without our consent. We had nothing to do with it anymore."

The pinpoint of light expanded to a flashlight beam.

"That helps," I said, without much enthusiasm.

"You will handle this, Herr Furst?"

"Yes."

"Why are they doing this? If they want to sue me they can sue me, but why are they trying to spoil my loan?"

"Because they know they have a bad case."

"Herr Furst, I do not follow this explanation."

"They know that if they simply sue Schellenwerk on the guaranty, they'll eventually lose. They hope that by holding the loan hostage they'll persuade you to throw some money at them tomorrow morning to make them go away."

"*Nein!*" the Teutonic syllable thundered through the Atlantic cable. "Never! We will pay nothing. I do not care if the entire loan goes kaput."

That's when I panicked.

Chapter Eight

Shortly before 5:15, Thomas and Sandy left their apartment to walk to Campagna, one of those unpretentious little Italian restaurants that you used to be able to find about every third block in Manhattan. There they enjoyed lasagne, veal marsala, garlic bread, Chianti and a couple of leisurely Caporals before Thomas's limousine picked them up to drive them to the ball game.

That was why there wasn't any answer when in a cold sweat I called their apartment shortly after getting off the phone with Joachim Schellen. And why there wasn't any answer thirty seconds later on the car phone in Thomas's limousine. As it turned out, in fact, it was nearly nine o'clock that night before I finally managed to reach them. During the intervening three hours and forty-five minutes, they had a much better time at Campagna and the Polo Grounds than I did at the office.

I should explain something about the Polo Grounds. Before there was a baseball stadium there, the Polo Grounds really was a huge, rectangular field where people played polo. Baseball fields are called diamonds but of course they aren't diamond-shaped at all. A baseball field is a right triangle whose hypotenuse is a curve instead of a straight line. Back when they were built the way they're supposed to be, baseball stadiums followed the configuration of the fields they surrounded.

Superimposing this design on an immense rectangle made the Polo Grounds a distinctive stadium. For one thing, a muscular high-schooler could knock the ball out of the park down the right-field line, whereas King Kong would've had a tough time hitting a home run to center. For another, there were blind spots from almost anywhere you sat in the stadium.

Almost. From the press box you could see just about anywhere on the field of play. At a time when luxury boxes were virtually unknown and the best seat money could buy was a hardwood chair exposed to rain, cold, and passing drunks, a place in the press box at the Polo Grounds was every bit as special as Fielder had advertised it.

Thomas and Sandy got to the stadium around seven-forty and worked their way up the concrete ramp to the concession level in between the lower and upper grandstands. Chain-link fence guarded the drop from this level onto the seats below. Long, narrow walkways bridged this drop at wide intervals, allowing limited access from the concession area to the press box.

Thomas and Sandy presented their passes at the gate to the first walkway they came to, just to the right of the home plate area. An aging, sallow-faced usher guarding the gate examined the documents with an expression at once bored and baffled.

"What's this?" he asked himself irritably.

"Jerry Fielder's party," Thomas said.

With this hint the gatekeeper apparently puzzled the mystery out. He jerked his thumb in the general direction of the right field foul pole.

"Last gate," he said.

"Welcome to New York," Thomas remarked as he and Sandy began their hike in the indicated direction. The gatekeeper shrugged.

The last gate was about twenty yards past first base. The Mets were willing to let Fielder have press box seats in exchange for a substantial group purchase and a little pull, but they had no intention of letting his party actually sit anywhere near the broadcasters and writers who really belonged there. It looked to Thomas as if an acre or so of impassable space would separate them from the legitimate press box denizens.

Another usher, every bit as enthusiastic as his colleague, sat at a rickety card table just outside the walkway. He examined their passes, grunted in what Thomas took to be grudging acquiescence in their right to be there, and turned an ancient, battered three-ring binder toward them. The binder was opened to a loose-leaf page with a log-in matrix inked onto it.

"Print your name on the first clear line and put down what time you're coming in," he instructed them in a monotone.

Thomas and Sandy obeyed.

"Seven forty-five," Thomas murmured as he glanced impressionistically at his watch.

"Seven forty-eight," Sandy corrected him as she looked carefully at hers.

Sandy noticed that they were the eighth and ninth people to sign in.

Fielder spotted them when they were still twenty feet from the top of the walkway.

"Hey, straighten up, crew," he yelled into the press box. "We got some class comin' on board. Come on up here, Currys, there's some people I wancha to meet."

The walkway led into the second-last section of the press box, where a pastrami and roast beef buffet that covered the section-long desk had attracted most of the party. The room was low-ceilinged, about thirty feet long and only eight feet or so wide. At its right end (the end nearer the foul pole), R.J. stood impassively at the closed door to the end section. At its left end (the end nearer first base) a door stood ajar, inviting any spillover from the buffet into the next section—the last one open to Fielder's party. The door at the other end of that section looked securely locked, and bore a sign sternly forbidding anyone even to think about coming through it.

Through the open doorway Thomas could see someone on his knees, chipping aggressively at the ice that surrounded canned beer and bottled Coke in a cooler on the floor there. He noticed a single, tiny restroom in the left rear corner of the section they had entered.

"Where's Mary Margaret?" their host bawled at R.J. "Didn't you bring her in?"

"She stopped at a pay phone to check up on things at home."

"There's a phone right on the ramp here she could use for free."

"She didn' know that, Jer."

"You've already met Harry Liebniewicz," Fielder said then to Thomas and Sandy, nodding toward the Teamsters operative. "That's his wife Ginny with him."

Virginia Liebniewicz looked around and bobbed her head toward Thomas and Sandy. She was nearly as tall as her husband, her close-cropped dark hair streaked with gray. Holding a sandwich in one hand and a paper cup of coffee in the other, she seemed in no particular hurry to wipe away the driblet of mustard that trailed from the right corner of her lips.

Fielder herded Thomas and Sandy farther along the section, toward the first-base end.

"You haven't met these two gentlemen," he said, "but I think TAC may've heard one of their names this mornin'."

He guided them to a knot near the doorway where two men and one woman were standing. The woman looked to be in her middle twenties. She was wearing a taxicab-yellow dress with black trim that showed off her deeply suntanned face and shoulders and her brilliant blond hair to good advantage. She was smoking a cigarette that she held in a six-inch black holder. Everything works, Thomas thought, except the holder. Audrey Hepburn using a cigarette holder in *Breakfast at Tiffany's* looked cosmopolitan. This woman using one at the Polo Grounds looked like a twit.

The taller of the two men stood at the woman's left, his elbow brushing her bicep with confident familiarity. He was just over six feet tall and looked as if he weighed close to two hundred solid pounds. His blue eyes suggested the zesty vitality of someone who hasn't yet seen his fortieth birthday or felt his first real intimations of mortality, but at his temples his black hair had already given way to white.

The other man was closer to Sandy's height. Whatever color his hair was, he was losing it fast. He held a cup of clear soda with the thumbs and first two fingers of both hands, directly in front of the top button on his vest. His tie was Persian blue with thick, black diagonal stripes. Speaking in an accent that was about halfway between stage English and Back Bay, he was completing a comment to the woman as Fielder approached.

". . . doesn't necessarily prove anything, you see. Because if, say, you set a hundred thousand monkeys at typewriters, just pounding the keys at random, you see, why in a million years or so they'd produce works of Shakespeare."

"If you set a hundred thousand monkeys at typewriters," the other man said in the kind of tone engineers use when they talk to interior decorators, "in sixteen hours they'd run out of ribbon, and in seventeen hours you'd have a hundred thousand typewriters ready for the scrap heap."

"Looks like I got here just in time," Fielder said. "I'd like you folks to meet Thomas an' Sandy Curry. TAC an' Mrs. Curry, the big one's Andy Birnham, an' the little fella's B. Weldon Corbett."

Birnham nodded. Corbett trusted his drink to his left hand

long enough to shake hands briefly with Thomas and Sandy. Fielder glanced at the woman.

"I'm terribly sorry, darlin'," he said, "but I forgot your name already."

"I'm Natalie Underwood. I'm with Andy."

"Happy to meet you," Thomas said. "I think I heard somewhere that Mr. Corbett is involved in retailing. Are you two competitors by any chance?"

Birnham shook his head. "I own Long Island Trucking, Warehouse, and Storage," he said.

"Cor-Mart Appliances and Electronics is my company," Corbett said. "Fourteen outlets in the four-state area, six in metropolitan New York alone. Growing all the time."

"That's exactly what I heard this morning," Thomas said. "About how you're growing, I mean."

Corbett beamed.

"There's Mary Margaret," Fielder yelped happily as he looked over his shoulder. "C'mover here, sunshine," he called. He wrapped his arm almost shyly around the shoulders of a short, stocky, round-faced woman when she came up. "I want you to meet Thomas an' Sandy Curry."

"Pleasure," the woman said, shaking hands with each of them. She was holding a copy of *The Life of Christ* by Bishop Fulton J. Sheen, a featured selection of the Doubleday Book Club that year. She had marked her place with last Sunday's copy of *The Tablet*, the weekly newspaper of the New York archdiocese.

"Mary Margaret's a teacher," Fielder said proudly. "Second grade at Mary Queen of Heaven."

"A teacher," said Sandy, who came from a country where such a position implied a specific educational background and entailed considerable status. "What college did you attend?"

"School of Hard Knocks," Mary Margaret said, smiling evenly. "When I left Visitation High School, I knew how to type, take shorthand, and file things in alphabetical order. I expected to be a secretary. You don't need a college degree for that."

"But you became an instructor instead?"

"Yeah. Parochial school teaching doesn't pay as well as secretarial work, but you don't need a college degree for that, either, and it gives me a chance to be near the kids."

"Okay," Fielder said. "That takes carra the introductions. If you two hustle you can get somethin' to eat before they play 'The Star Spangled Banner' an' then we can watch ourselves a baseball game. Everybody have a good time."

Sandy was more interested in writing the starting lineups down in her scorebook than she was in eating a second dinner. As soon as a harried concessionaire had cleared enough of the buffet away to make some desk space, Sandy sat down with Thomas, opened her scorebook, and went to work.

By the time the game actually started, everyone else had found seats as well. Birnham sat at the first-base end of what had been the buffet section, about ten feet from Thomas and Sandy. He seemed to watch the play on the field the way he might watch "The Dick Van Dyke Show," with a kind of detached half-interest, as though it were white noise that mildly engaged his attention while permitting him to think about other things. Natalie Underwood sat next to him, paging deliberately through Jack Paar's memoirs, *My Saber Is Bent.*

Frank Bolling led off for the Braves by hitting a 2-1 pitch solidly toward left. Elio Chacon, the Mets' shortstop, took one step to his right and caught the line drive on the fly. The crowd cheered, some of the applause representing mean-spirited sarcasm but most if it reflecting genuinely delighted surprise at this display of journeyman competence.

In her scorebook, Sandy wrote "6" in the box opposite Bolling's name for the first inning.

Harry and Ginny Liebniewicz sat about halfway between Thomas and Sandy and the far end of the section. They watched the game in synch, exchanging comments on each pitch.

Roy McMillan slapped a ground ball directly at the Mets' first baseman, Marv Throneberry. Throneberry fielded the ball cleanly and tossed it to Roger Craig, pitching again for the Mets, who raced over to cover first base. McMillan was fast, but the play was routine and he was out by a step.

Sandy wrote "3-1" in the first-inning box opposite McMillan's name.

"Craig's pitching a good game," Ginny Liebniewicz said.

"No-hitter through two-thirds of an inning," her husband agreed, his voice as ironic as hers.

Corbett began by sitting just beyond the Liebniewiczes. In diction that didn't fit particularly well with his accent, he undertook an extended monologue in an unsuccessful effort to engage them in conversation.

"Union guy, huh? I think that's terrific, I really do. I am one hundred percent a supporter of the American labor movement. I have no problem with unions, let me tell you. And I mean that. Now fair's fair, I have to say that. I mean, what I mean is, five bucks an hour for skilled labor— absolutely. The workman is worthy of his hire, that's what I say. Some guy, on the other hand, you see, some guy popping the same hole thirty times an hour in a strip of sheet metal, I have yet to meet the guy can explain to me how that's worth four seventy-five an hour. I mean, that's not an artisan, you see, that's not a craftsman, that's just semiskilled labor, and I see no reason why—"

Harry Liebniewicz turned expressionlessly toward Corbett. He held up the index and little fingers of his left hand.

"What's that?" he asked.

"I'll bite," Corbett said. "What is it?"

"That's a punch-press operator ordering four beers." Corbett looked blank for a moment. Then his mouth opened and closed once. "See," Liebniewicz continued, "that's two reasons right there."

Henry Aaron hit a line drive over Charlie Neal's head into right field. He rounded first and went back to the bag as

Richie Ashburn retrieved the ball and threw it to Chacon at second.

In the first-inning box opposite Aaron's name, Sandy circled "1b," drew a line from home plate to first base, and drew a second line from home plate to the middle of right field.

R.J. sat at the far end of the press box section. Jerry and Mary Margaret Fielder had gone into the last section and closed the door.

Eddie Mathews hit the ball up the middle, just to the first-base side of second. Neal scooted over it, backhanded it, staggered, recovered, and flipped the ball to Chacon covering second in time to force out Aaron.

Opposite Mathews' name Sandy wrote "FC 4-6." Fielder's choice, second to short. Then she went down to the summary box at the bottom of the column for the first inning. A diagonal line slashed through the box. Above the line she wrote "0." Below the line she wrote "1." No runs on one hit for the Braves in the first inning.

During the break between the top and bottom of the first inning, Thomas looked around as someone new came into the press box. He appeared to be in his fifties, bald and peppery, bustling into the section. R.J. glanced up at the entrance.

"Hi, Mr. Kovacs," he called.

"Hi, kid. Where's Jerry?"

"I'll tell him you're here."

"Tell him I'm sorry I'm late, willya? The traffic was just murder coming over here."

Kovacs strode up and down the length of the press box section, his watery blue eyes unbashfully appraising each of the people there in turn. R.J. knocked on the door to the end section, waited a moment, then opened the door and went in.

"No damage yet?" Kovacs asked, apparently of the room in general.

"Shutout through the top of the first," Harry Liebniewicz said. "Why don't you pull up a chair and stay awhile?"

"Sitting too much makes me nervous."

"Pacing makes me nervous."

"Maybe you're right."

Kovacs sat in the chair immediately to Sandy's left and began typing on an imaginary keyboard on the desk.

R.J. came out of the end section. He walked to where Corbett was sitting and spoke briefly in a low voice to the appliance and electronics retailer. Corbett got up and walked through the doorway into the end section. After making sure that the door closed securely behind Corbett, R.J. resumed his seat in the chair just outside that door.

The Mets' half of the first inning was by now underway. Lew Burdette, the Braves' pitcher, threw four pitches to Charlie Neal. Neal didn't swing at any of them. Three of them were strikes.

Sandy wrote "K" in the first inning box opposite Neal's name.

"Enjoying the game?" Thomas asked Kovacs.

"So far."

"My name's Curry," Thomas said, reaching behind Sandy to offer his hand to Kovacs. "Pleased to meet you."

"Louie Kovacs," Kovacs said. He shook Thomas's hand briefly, without taking his eyes off the field. "You friends a Jerry's?"

"Ever since he gave Sandy his scorebook and turned her into a baseball fanatic a few weeks ago," Thomas said.

Burdette threw four pitches to Felix Mantilla. Mantilla swung at three of them. He didn't hit any.

Sandy wrote "K" in the first inning box opposite Mantilla's name.

"Burdette looks tough tonight," Ginny Liebniewicz said.

"Against the Mets your kid sister'd look tough," Harry Liebniewicz commented.

Burdette threw one pitch to Richie Ashburn. Ashburn swung and hit it on the ground to Bolling, the Braves' second baseman. Without difficulty Bolling threw Ashburn out at first.

Sandy wrote "4-3" opposite Ashburn's name in the first-inning column. Then she put two zeroes in the summary box.

Corbett came out of the end section and resumed his seat. Following him out, R. J. walked the length of the section to speak briefly and in low tones to Birnham. Birnham whispered something to his companion, then rose and strode toward the end section. The door closed behind him.

"Hey, kid—" Kovacs said to R.J.

"Sure, Mr. Kovacs. Anything you want to eat or drink?"

"I'll letcha know. What I want right now—"

"Sure, Mr. Kovacs."

R.J. resumed his seat just outside the door to the end section.

Hm, Thomas thought to himself.

Leading off the second for the Braves, Joe Adcock hit a towering fly ball, slicing toward the right field corner. Richie Ashburn ran it down and caught it nonchalantly at shoulder level. Sandy wrote "9" in her scorebook.

Del Crandall walked on six pitches. Sandy circled "BB" for "base on balls" and drew a line from home plate to first base.

Lee Maye lined the first pitch down the third base line and into the left field corner. Crandall slid into third. Maye cruised into second. Sandy drew lines from first to second and from second to third for Crandall, circled "2b" for Maye, drew a line from home plate to left field, and drew lines from home plate to first and first to second.

Gus Bell hit a 2-2 pitch to medium center field. Jim Hickman caught the ball. Crandall tagged at third and chugged home after the catch. Hickman shrugged and threw the ball to third, holding Maye at second.

Sandy drew a line from third to home for Crandall. Opposite Bell's name she wrote, "SF 8 RBI" and circled "SAC." Sacrifice fly to the center fielder. Run batted in. No at-bat charged to the hitter.

Burdette struck out on a 1-2 pitch. Sandy put a "K" opposite his name and put "1/1" in the second-inning summary box for the Braves. One run on one hit.

Birnham came out of the end section and sat back down next to Natalie Underwood.

"Do you suppose it's our turn to go in?" Thomas asked Sandy.

"I beg your pardon?" Sandy hadn't been paying attention to anything but the game.

"It looks like our host is holding little private conferences in the end section down there, one guest at a time. First Corbett went in and came back, then Birnham. I was just wondering if we were next."

"Do you attach significance to this?" Sandy asked.

"Hard to say."

R.J. whispered a few words to Liebniewicz. Liebniewicz got up and walked toward the end section.

"This isn't really the most compatible group you could imagine, is it?" Thomas asked.

"What do you mean?"

"I mean there isn't really a lot of mixing going on. This isn't so much a party as eleven people who happen to be within fifty feet of each other."

"I am enjoying it very much," Sandy said.

The Mets came up in the bottom of the second. Marv Throneberry led off.

"The point is," Thomas said to Sandy, "if the reason we were all invited here wasn't to have a good time with each other, what was the reason?"

Throneberry hit Burdette's third pitch high and deep to right. It curved foul just before going into the seats. Burdette missed with the next two pitches and Throneberry trotted to first base. Sandy made the appropriate notations in her scorebook.

"What do you think accounts for it, then?" Sandy asked when she had finished.

"I don't really know. I'd hate to think that you and I are being used to provide an alibi to someone for something that's supposed to happen tonight before this ball game's over, but you can't really rule it out, can you?"

Frank Thomas bunted the ball weakly toward the right side of the infield. Burdette pounced off the mound and fielded the ball. He glanced at second, saw that he had no play there, and threw to first to retire Thomas as Throneberry advanced.

"One cannot really rule out anything unless one has enough facts," Sandy said as she recorded a 1-3 sacrifice for the batter and showed Throneberry moving up to second base. "On the other hand, not being able to rule a conclusion out hardly justifies jumping to that conclusion, does it?"

"I suppose not. But it might justify an effort to mingle with our host if this goes on much longer."

Jim Hickman chopped the ball in between third and short. Mathews, the Braves' third baseman, cut in front of McMillan to field the ball, brought it up in his glove, and then watched it squirt out of the mitt and fall back to the infield dirt. Sandy drew a line from second to third for Throneberry and put Hickman at first with the notation "E-5."

"Heads up," Thomas said. "For the Mets this qualifies as a rally. They can tie the score with a halfway decent fly ball."

Chacon hit a ground ball three feet to McMillan's right.

"Double play," Thomas groaned, slapping the desk.

Fielding the ball cleanly, McMillan pegged it to second where Bolling caught it and pivoted expertly so that he could throw the ball to first and complete the double play. Instead of doing that, however, he fell over on his backside as Hickman rolled into him and Throneberry crossed the plate.

"FC 6-4 RBI," Sandy noted in her scorebook.

"Walk, unintentional sacrifice bunt, error, fielder's choice. It's a lot more creative way to score than a home run, isn't it?" Thomas asked.

"More interesting to record also," Sandy said.

The next batter, Chris Cannizzaro, hit a fly ball to center field that Lee Maye caught. Sandy wrote "8" in the second-inning box next to Cannizzaro's name and "1/0" in the summary box at the bottom: one run on no hits.

Harry Liebniewicz came back and resumed his seat.

"Time to mingle a little more thoroughly and see if I can find out what's going on," Thomas said to Sandy.

"Thomas—" Sandy began dubiously.

"Excuse me, folks." Thomas and Sandy looked up at R.J.'s voice. "Jerry was wondering if you'd mind joining him down in the end section there."

"You talked us into it," Thomas said.

"Hey, kid," Kovacs interjected irritably from a yard away. "What—"

"Sure, you too, Mr. Kovacs."

"Maybe if we're good we can solo next season," Thomas whispered to Sandy.

"Behave," Sandy admonished him with mock severity.

Fielder greeted them as they stepped back into the last section of the press box.

"Hey, everybody come on in," he called out. "Find a seat an' we'll have R.J. volunteer to do a beer run. How's everybody enjoyin' the game?"

"I was pretty nervous there for a minute," Kovacs said while chairs scraped on the plate-metal floor of the press box. "Tell ya the truth, I'm still a little nervous."

"Well, Louie, you always have been a kind of a nervous guy, haven't ya?" Fielder responded. Kovacs had sat next to the door. Fielder took the next seat, in between Kovacs and Mary Margaret. He squared his own scorecard on the desk in front of him.

"Tell me something, Jerry," Kovacs said. "Do I have anything to be nervous about?"

"You need anything to be nervous about?" Fielder asked.

"Jerry, you keep answering a question with a question."

"That's what micks do, Louie. That's one of the four things micks do. We marry late, we eat fish on Friday, we drink on Saturday, an' we answer a question with a question. Which reminds me of somethin'. R.J., why did God allow beer to be invented?"

"So that the Irish wouldn't rule the world," R.J. answered instantly.

"So?"

"I'm on my way."

Bolling had by this time stepped to the plate to lead off the third inning for the Braves. He hit the ball in the same place he'd hit it in the first inning, but five feet higher. It soared over Chacon's glove and bounced on the grass well into left field.

"Nervous, Louie?" Fielder asked as he scratched at his scorecard.

"Leadoff hitter on and heavy lumber coming up, what've I got to be nervous about?" Kovacs demanded. "What's goin' on, Jerry?"

"Piece a' cake, Louie. Don't sweat it. The cat's in the bag an' the bag's in the river."

McMillan swung at the first pitch and smashed the ball on two hops over third base. Mantilla dove to his left and gloved the ball when it was all but past him. Still on his knees he whipped the ball to Neal at second who caught it, pivoted, and threw out McMillan at first.

As Sandy wrote "DP 5-4-3" in her scorebook she glanced at Kovacs and Fielder. Kovacs's face was pale and his lips were trembling. Fielder's eyes were luminous.

Not secretively, exactly, but also without really advertising what he was doing, Fielder passed Kovacs a small custard-colored window envelope, the sort bills often came in back then. Kovacs opened it, glanced at its contents, then slipped it without comment into the right side pocket of his coat.

"Okay, Jerry," he said. He stood up and headed for the door.

"You're welcome for the hospitality, Louie," Fielder said just before Kovacs stalked out.

Over the next nine minutes, five things happened: Hank Aaron singled to right; Eddie Mathews doubled to right center, with Aaron stopping at third; the Mets walked Adcock intentionally; the public address announcer asked that Thomas Andrew Curry call the stadium operator; and Del Crandall flied out to center field.

"No runs, three hits, no errors, three left on," Fielder said. "What'd I tell Louie? Nothin' to sweat, right?"

Thomas didn't hear that because he was on the way to the telephone behind the ramp door at the rear of the next section. He called the stadium operator, who relayed the message I'd left for him and Sandy: I NEED YOUR HELP.

Chapter Nine

"Thomas, I need a case. I need a case that says, point blank, crime and guarantors don't pay."

"Could you be a bit more specific?"

"The case has to say that if you do anything—*anything*—to increase the risk on a guaranteed debt, the guarantor's off the hook. I need a case that hits that proposition right across the seams, right on the numbers, so dead bang on point that Judge Sims won't have to do any reasoning at all."

"None at all? Not even a two-term syllogism?"

"None at all. I need to be able to stand up at eight tomorrow morning and say, 'May it please the Court, *Smith* v. *Jones,* I win.' Judge Sims isn't going to have the inclination or the capacity to handle anything more complicated than that."

Thomas sat across my desk from me and nodded. It was about 9:25 P.M. Thomas and Sandy had signed hurriedly out of the press box at the Polo Grounds a little over half an hour before.

Sandy was in her own office trying to transform an indignant German cable into a coherent English affidavit. Mrs. Walbach was at her desk, cutting and pasting typescript to put together the third version of the statement of facts in our brief. The rest of our brief wasn't written yet, and it wasn't going to get written until Thomas came up with the dream case I'd just described to him.

"All right," he said. "I'll see what I can do."

He got up and headed for the offices of Leverett, Leverett & Means, an insurance defense firm upstairs from Curry & Furst that boasted a law library much more complete than ours.

I was glad he hadn't asked me the obvious questions: Weren't any of the lawyers employed on a full-time basis by Curry & Furst familiar with the rudiments of legal research? Was it really necessary to pull a free-lancer like Thomas away from a baseball game for a project like this? I was glad he didn't ask these questions because the most plausible answer to them was that perhaps Theodore Furst had punched the panic button.

The real answer was a little more complicated than that. I had panicked all right, but my reaction to the panic had a solid foundation. There was something very special about the way Thomas approached a legal problem.

There are two kinds of lawyers: counsellors and advocates. Counsellors start with a question and come up with an answer based on what the law is. Advocates start with the answer—my client should win—and come up with law to back that answer up. Advocates look on counsellors about the way the marines look on the army: down. Thomas was an advocate with a special instinct for the jugular, a sixth sense about the shortest, sharpest way to close for the kill. That's what I needed the night of September 26.

I had one hold over Thomas that I didn't have over anyone else in the world: I was the only way he could practice law. He had voluntarily surrendered his law license a couple of years before. His reasons for doing so were quite honorable, but that didn't change the fact that he no longer had the legal right to act as an attorney. If he wanted to work on real-world legal problems, he had to find a tractable member of the bar who needed him and knew it. I qualified.

There was only one limitation on this hold I had over Thomas: I could never use it. If I'd ever even tried to extract any cooperation from him by hinting that if he didn't come across he'd be out of the unofficial attorney business, he'd have walked away for good—just as he'd surrendered his law license rather than let anyone think they could use the threat of losing it to control him. When I wanted him to do something, all I could do was say what I said on September 26: I need your help.

After Thomas took off for the library I wandered out to Mrs. Walbach's desk to see how the cut-and-paste effort was going. We didn't have word processors in 1962. If you wanted to change three words on a page of text, you didn't just bring it up on a screen, make the changes, and have a laser printer bang out a new page at twelve words a second. You did the job with scissors and tape and a photocopier, and you hoped for the best.

Mrs. Walbach was very good at this. When I got to her desk she was working on the last two pages of the statement of facts. I started proofreading the first six that she'd already finished. She handed page seven to me as I finished page five. I had to wait ninety seconds after I got to the bottom of page seven for her to hand me page eight.

They were flawless. We had a nice, crisp, letter-perfect factual statement. Now all we needed was an argument.

Sandy came down the corridor toward us. She wasn't running, exactly, but she wasn't wasting any time either.

She handed me a dozen pages of quadrille-lined lab-report paper covered with her straightforward, no-nonsense longhand. I read the first page, changed half a dozen words, and handed it to Mrs. Walbach. Her typewriter's staccato rattle seemed to start instantly.

I had the entire draft revised and ready for her by the time the first page was out of the typewriter. Sandy picked up the first typed page and started proofreading. She could do that as well as I could. It was 10:15 by now and I decided to go see how Thomas was doing.

There were a dozen attorneys in the library even at that hour, but I spotted Thomas instantly. He was sitting alone at a round table of honey-colored oak. A green-shaded fixture cast a circle of intense light on the volume he had open before him and three other volumes, also open and piled on top of each other, that lay just beyond it.

It seemed to me that he was reading the text with the intensity of someone who thought he was onto something, but I told myself that that might be just wishful thinking. I walked up slowly behind him, careful not to disturb his concentration. I was about six feet away when I saw his shoulders stiffen slightly.

"Gotcha," he whispered to himself.

"Something helpful?" I asked.

He whipped around sharply.

"Oh, hello, Theodore," he said. "I have your case for you."

"That's welcome news." I sat down about forty degrees around the table from him. "Tell me about it."

"*Camp* v. *Albany Trust*," he said. "Four people sign a guaranty of payment of a corporate debt. Beneath one of the signatures someone types, 'Limited to value of stock owned.' "

"Beneath just one of the signatures?"

"Right."

"When was the limitation put on there?"

"That was the issue at trial," Thomas said. "The bank said the limiting language was on there before anyone signed. The guarantors claimed it was put on after everyone had signed and that the three who weren't limited hadn't known anything about it."

"Swearing contest."

"Wrong. The guarantors came up with a document examination expert who produced a back-lighted blowup of the signature block showing the typestrokes of the 't' and the 'd' in 'Limited' and the 'k' in 'stock' overlying the pen stroke of part of the limited guarantor's signature."

"Proving that the signature was on the document before the limiting language was."

"Correct," Thomas said. "Which in turn proved, in the considered opinion of a majority of the New York Court of Appeals, that the guaranty wasn't worth the paper it was written on as far as the other guarantors were concerned."

"Because the limitation increased their risk without their consent."

"Right."

"Which is exactly what happened to Schellenwerk when the principal debtor's collateral was released after the refinancing."

"Right."

"So we win."

"So it would appear, Theodore."

"Let's go downstairs."

I listened to Thomas dictate the argument while Mrs. Walbach finished the corrections to the affidavit. As soon as she was through with those Thomas gave her the Dictabelt he'd been using so that she could start typing from it, and continued his dictation on a fresh one. By shortly after 11:30 he was through. From the point we'd reached I figured we'd get to a complete and presentable brief in three more hours.

"All right, Thomas," I said, "thank you very much. I truly appreciate this. Mrs. Walbach and I can take it from here."

"Theodore, don't be ridiculous."

"Excuse me, Thomas?"

"Theodore, you have to be in court a little over eight hours from now. After you get through in court, you have to take care of a loan closing that could last all afternoon and into the evening."

"It goes with the territory, Thomas."

"That isn't the point. Everything from here on in is mechanical. Mrs. Walbach and Sandy and I will take care of it. You will go downstairs where my car will pick you up and take you to your club so that you can get a few hours' sleep, shave, take a shower and be out front at seven-fifteen tomorrow morning. We will pick you up then with the brief and affidavit ready to go and something nutritious and portable for you to have for breakfast, and get you to court."

I hesitated. He was right, of course. The problem was that for most of the time I'd known him Thomas had tended to approach law (and life) with a kind of ironic detachment. This occasionally produced the kind of free-spirited outbursts—limericks in briefs, for example—that seem just marvelous when you do them but that turn out not to go over very well in court at eight in the morning. What Thomas was saying between the lines of his dogmatic pronouncement was that he was willing to impersonate a grown-up until this crisis was over, and did I trust him to bring it off?

"You're right," I said. "I'll see you tomorrow at seven-fifteen."

At seven-fifteen on the dot the following morning I climbed into Thomas's limousine. He handed me a fried-egg-and-bacon sandwich on wholewheat toast while Sandy put beside me on the seat a neat little package with the end results of the night's efforts: an original and three copies of a fifteen-page brief and a five-page affidavit, complete with notarized certificates of telephonic authentication and correct translation, all stapled into correctly captioned, stiff, blue construction paper backings.

Thomas and Sandy had a feverish kind of shine in their eyes. Part of it was the physical disorientation that comes with unusual fatigue. They'd each been up for around twenty-four hours. Another part of it, though, was excitement and pride. People know when they've done something above and beyond the call of duty, something that in its own quiet way is heroic. It's a good feeling, and I'd almost have traded my good night's sleep for the right to share it.

68

We were in court by 7:55. I had the satisfaction of seeing a look of unpleasant surprise wash over the face of opposing counsel when I handed him his copies of our pleadings. Judge Sims listened to us in bored patience for fifteen minutes, retired to his chambers long enough to read our brief and *Camp* v. *Albany Trust*, and denied the plaintiff's motion at 8:40. By ten minutes of nine we were headed back to midtown.

"Congratulations," Thomas said. "You can go ahead with your closing."

"And you and Sandy can get some sleep."

"The thought had crossed our minds," Sandy said.

September 27

BARNETT AIDE, IN SCUFFLE, BARS
NEGRO FROM U. OF MISSISSIPPI;
GOVERNOR REJECTS COURT NOTICE
New York Times, September 27, 1962, p. 1, col. 5

HEAD OF TEAMSTERS LOCAL IS HELD
IN EMBEZZLEMENT
New York Times, September 27, 1962, p. 17, col. 3

MIG NEARLY HITS U.S. BERLIN PLANE
New York Times, September 27, 1962, p. 1, col. 2

CUBA FIRING SQUADS REPORTED
KILLING 75 FOR ANTI-CASTRO PLOT
New York Times, September 27, 1962, p. 9, col. 3

A Federal District judge ruled today that betting on a sure thing did not violate the antigambling statute. . . . "However nefarious, the scheme did not involve the element of chance," the judge said.
New York Times, September 27, 1962, p. 39, col. 3

Chapter Ten

Detective-Lieutenant Herschel Bernstein, as he introduced himself, was five feet, ten inches tall and had packed 165 pounds onto a medium frame with only a little bulge here and there. He was forty-eight years old and Thomas thought he looked every day of it—indeed, that he had probably looked forty-eight when he was twenty-one, the kind of guy who'd asked for a briefcase for his ninth birthday. He had a bushy, salt-and-pepper moustache and thick eyebrows to match. Tiny pinpoints of iridescent red and blue seemed to stand out in the zigzag weave of his gray suit.

"I'm sorry you had to learn about Mr. Fielder's death this way," he said as he stepped into the Curry apartment. "But I guess there isn't any good way."

"I suppose not," Thomas said.

It was just after four o'clock on September 27. After Bernstein's call from downstairs Thomas had hastily pulled on a polo shirt and khaki slacks and gone out to greet the detective while Sandy finished dressing.

"How long had you known him?" Bernstein asked.

"Not long. Let me think. Come in and sit down."

"Thank you."

"Let's see. Less than a month. We didn't meet until Sandy and I got back from our honeymoon. Would you like a drink?"

"No thanks. This is Mrs. Curry?"

Thomas looked and saw Sandy walk into the apartment's living room. She was wearing a pale blue blouse and a flannel skirt. Thomas and Bernstein both stood. Thomas introduced his wife.

"Enchanted to make your acquaintance. How was Jerry killed?" Sandy demanded, dispensing with any further niceties.

"He was stabbed through the heart with an ice pick," Bernstein said after an intrigued glance at Sandy.

"When?"

"His scorecard for the game was filled out through the top of the eighth inning. An usher found his body about eleven-fifteen, a little better than twenty minutes after the game ended."

"Do you have any idea who did this?" It was still Sandy asking.

Bernstein sat back down in the tufted leather chair he had chosen and slouched slightly to the right.

"I suppose that depends on what you mean by 'any idea,' " he said slowly. "You had to have a pass to get into that part of the press box. Ten people besides Jerry Fielder had passes for that night and signed in for that area. Two of those people are you and Mr. Curry. So if neither of you did it, there's a pretty good chance it was one of the other eight."

"What can we do to help you find out which one it was?"

"Start by telling me when you left the game."

"Just before nine," Thomas said.

"Eight fifty-three," Sandy said at the same time. They

looked at each other. "I checked my watch when we signed out," she explained. "One had to sign one's name on exiting and note the time one was leaving."

"Can you remember who else was there?"

"Well, let's see," Thomas said. "Jerry and his wife and R.J., of course. And us. That's five."

"Yes," Sandy said. She pressed the first two fingers of each hand to her temples and closed her eyes. "There was Harry Liebniewicz," she added finally. "And his wife."

"Right," Thomas said. "Jean or Jeannie or something."

"Ginny."

"That was it. Short for Virginia."

"And then there was the very nervous man. Jerry kept calling him Louie."

"Do you remember his last name?" Bernstein asked.

Sandy shook her head.

"I don't remember the names of the others either," Thomas said. "Two men and one woman. One of the men was in retailing. Appliances or something. The other one was involved in some way with a warehouse."

Bernstein nodded.

"Kovacs," Thomas said suddenly, snapping his fingers. "That was Louie's last name. It just came to me."

"That's pretty good," Bernstein said. "I meet somebody at a party, I can't remember his name five minutes later. Did anyone leave before you did?"

"Only Kovacs," Thomas said.

"Well," Sandy interjected, "this Kovacs man left the part of the press box where we were sitting a few minutes before Thomas and I left, and we did not see him again. But we did not actually see him leave. Leave the entire press box, I mean."

"Precision," Thomas said to Bernstein, indicating Sandy with his head. "Ask her what the principal export of Portugal is."

"Excuse me a second," Bernstein said. The slightest tincture of impatience colored his voice. "Do you mean you just didn't notice Kovacs leave the press box area, or do you mean that from where you were sitting you couldn't actually see whether he left the press box area or not?"

"The latter," Sandy answered instantly. "The nearest walkway from the stadium proper to the press box led to the middle of the three sections that Jerry was using for his party. Thomas and I spent most of our time at the game in that section. Shortly before we left, though, Jerry had R.J. ask us and this Kovacs into the end section, where Jerry and Mrs. Fielder were sitting. Kovacs walked out of that section and closed the door. We could not see where he went after that."

"Like you said," Bernstein commented to Thomas. "Precision."

"Speaking of which," Thomas said, "all this information Sandy and I—mostly Sandy, I'll admit—have been racking our brains trying to remember: Couldn't you get that from the sign-out sheet Sandy mentioned a while ago?"

"Yes and no," Bernstein said. "Someone made off with that sign-out sheet last night before the police got to the scene."

"That explains the no," Sandy said. "How about the yes?"

"About an hour before I left to come over here, someone delivered an unsealed white envelope to the precinct. No fingerprints on the envelope or its contents. Inside the envelope was a photocopy of the sign-out sheet."

Bernstein drew a folded sheet of slick paper from his inside coat pocket. He perched on the front edge of his chair, leaned over a glass-topped coffee table, and spread the page flat. Thomas and Sandy gathered on either side of him to examine it.

"Yes," Sandy said. "Seeing the names I remember them now. And the times agree with what I recall."

"Possibly," Bernstein said. "Or possibly seeing the information down here in black and white just makes you think you remember it that way."

"That's why you didn't just show us the sheet to start with," Thomas said.

DATE: SEPTEMBER 26, 1962

STATION: 3

	NAME (PLEASE PRINT)	TIME IN	TIME OUT	SIGNATURE (EXIT ONLY)
1	JERRY FIELDER	7:10		
2	RICK MADDEN	7:34	9:52	R.J. MADDON
3	ANDREW BIRNHAM	7:38	10:58	Andrew Birnham
4	Natalie Underwood	7:38	10:58	Natalie Underwood
5	HARRY L IEBNIEWICZ	7:42	10:49	Harry Liebniewicz
6	Virginia Liebniewicz	7:42	10:49	Virginy Liebniewicz
7	D. W. Corbett	7:45	9:35	Bradford Corbett
8	Thos. A. Curry	7:48	8:53	Thomas A. Curry
9	Sandrine Cadette Curry	7:48	8:53	Sandrine C. Curry
10	MARY MARGARET FIELDER	7:54	9:52	Mary Margaret Fielder
11	Louis J. Kovacs, Esq	8:15	9:40	Louis J. Kovacs, Esq
12				

"Right."

"Well and good," Sandy said. "But why did whoever went to the trouble to steal the sheet in the first place bother to make a photocopy to turn back over to the police? Or if someone else turned it over, how did that person get the original, and having done so why did that person then turn over a copy instead of the original?"

"Excellent questions," Bernstein said. "An obvious possible answer is that the original sheet was altered in some way to confuse the picture, throw suspicion in the wrong direction, protect the murderer in some way. The murderer may know that we can't ignore evidence that comes to us like this, even if we don't trust it. We have to follow up on it. And the more the follow-up squares with what the paper shows, the more conclusive the paper seems to become."

"If the murderer's trying to protect himself, that'd explain the photocopy," Thomas said. "An alteration would be harder to detect on a copy than on the original."

77

"Exactly. So that was why I said yes and no. Yes, I have a version of the sign-out sheet. But no, I can't necessarily rely on it."

"Look, Thomas," Sandy said. "This sheet says that Mrs. Fielder and R.J. left only about an hour after we did."

"And well before the game was over," Thomas noted.

"That matches their stories," Bernstein said. "Mrs. Fielder says that she got bored sometime around the fifth inning and decided to go home early. Her husband insisted that R.J. go with her and they left together after the sixth."

"Can the usher who was on duty verify any of the times?" Sandy asked.

"The district attorneys I've worked with have a saying, Mrs. Curry: If a witness hears a statement once, he thinks it might be true; if he hears it twice, he thinks it is true; and if he sees it in writing, you'll never convince him there's the slightest doubt about it."

"In other words, as far as the usher's concerned whatever's on this paper is gospel," Thomas said.

"Right again."

"So," Thomas said. "What else can we tell you?"

Bernstein moved his hips deeper into the chair and straightened slightly.

"You can tell me who'd want to kill Jerry Fielder and why." Sandy looked at Thomas.

"We don't have any hard information on that," Thomas said.

"Tell you what," Bernstein said. "You provide the information and I'll decide how hard it is."

"Let me put it this way," Thomas replied, choosing his words carefully. "Sandy and I didn't really know Jerry very well. We don't know what he did. From what little inkling I have of his activities, though, I'd say that if you didn't look at anything but possible motive you probably couldn't rule out anyone who was there that night. With the exception of Mrs. Fielder and Sandy."

"That's a very perceptive answer, Mr. Curry," Bernstein said. "Let *me* put it *this* way. I know a great deal about what Jerry Fielder did and how he did it. And based on what I know, I'd say that if you looked at possible motive alone you couldn't rule out anyone who was there that night, *including* Mrs. Fielder, yourself, and Mrs. Curry."

"Perhaps you'd better explain yourself," Thomas said.

"Yes," Bernstein said. "I think perhaps I'd better."

Chapter Eleven

"You ever read much about dinosaurs?" Bernstein asked. He had gotten up from his chair and was examining a large, busy painting titled *The Stump Orator* that hung over the couch.

"Not since I was nine," Thomas said.

"I've always been curious about them. Especially about why they died out. Did you know there are something like forty-six theories on that?"

"I never counted them."

"One of my favorites says it was early mammals. This scientist says these furry little mammals'd spend all their time hiding in the weeds till a couple of dinosaurs started fighting. Then, while the dinosaurs' attention was diverted, these mammals'd sneak out and feed on the dinosaurs' eggs. That Remington?" he asked, nodding toward the painting.

"George Caleb Bingham," Thomas said. "You were just getting to the part about Jerry."

"So I was." Bernstein turned around. He unbuttoned his suit coat and swept it back as he planted his hands on the back of his hips. "Jerry Fielder and I go back to the late forties. Jerry's modus operandi came straight from the early mammals. He'd wait until a couple of dinosaurs were fighting, then he'd sneak in and steal their eggs and be gone before they even knew anything was missing."

"Perhaps an example?" Sandy prompted.

"Fair enough. A little over four years ago two rich folks on their way home from the Heart Fund ball claimed they'd fallen in among thieves who relieved them of a diamond necklace insured for a hundred and five thousand dollars. The insurance company wondered why the wife had worn the real necklace out instead of the paste replica made for that purpose. They said they'd left the paste one in their Paris place when they'd flown back for this Heart Fund thing."

"The story's fishy but not absurd," Thomas said. "And juries dislike insurance companies even more than rich people, so I guess the insurer had to pay."

"It would've had to pay," Bernstein said, "except for a Catholic priest who came forward. He told the police that about two hours after the robbery he'd been called to the side of a man dying of a gunshot wound who was overwhelmed with remorse about helping to heist a necklace recently. To get absolved the repentant thief had to make restitution, so the priest was able to produce the stolen necklace."

"Which the insurance company returned to the couple, thereby avoiding payment of the claim," Thomas said. "And if the priest was telling the truth, what he turned over had to be what the thieves had taken from the couple."

"Exactly. And the priest was telling the truth. His story checked out, he aced the lie-detector test, and he indignantly rejected the finder's fee the insurance company offered him."

"As a result," Sandy said, "the presumed attempt to swindle the insurance company by passing off the theft of a paste necklace as the theft of a real one failed. But how did anyone except the insurance company come out ahead?"

"The couple found that out a month later when they quietly tried to peddle what they thought was the real necklace, which had been in Paris all the time. The dealer took one look at what they had and told them *it* was paste. Turned out that while they were in New York officially claiming the real necklace was there, someone was substituting a fake for the real necklace in Paris."

"But of course," Sandy said, smiling delightedly at the elegance of the undertaking. "The incompetent swindlers could do nothing whatever about it, because they had sworn a hundred oaths that the necklace in Paris was only paste anyway."

"Right."

"Okay," Thomas said. "But where did Jerry Fielder fit in?"

"Jerry did a very good job of impersonating a thief dying of a gunshot wound."

"What are you saying?" Sandy asked. "Had he been involved in the robbery, or hadn't he?"

"No. The robbery was a setup. The couple had offered to let the necklace be 'stolen' to pay off a gambling debt. The wife tried to double-cross everyone by wearing the replica when she was supposed to be wearing the genuine article. Fielder got wind of this thing, figured two dinosaurs were going at it and it's payday for him. He told the gambling debt creditor that if the necklace turned out to be phony he should call Jerry and Jerry'd save his hash. Early mammal."

"Okay," Thomas said. "Your point is that Jerry could've been pulling a fast one like that the night he was killed. Any or all of us could have been involved as collaborators or victims or both. Therefore, any one of us might've felt called upon to put an ice pick through his heart."

"We've been communicating, Mr. Curry. Now we approach the sixty-four-dollar question: What operation did

Jerry Fielder have going last night, and what was your role in it?"

"The answers to your questions in order are, we don't know and we don't know."

"Do you want us to find his killer?"

"Yes," Thomas said.

"*Evidemment*," Sandy said.

"It's not going to happen unless we can find some way to figure out what Jerry was up to just before he died. He didn't throw that party because he wanted to have a bunch of people watch a baseball game together. He had each of you there for a particular reason. Unless I can get a handle on that reason, Jerry's killer is going to get off scot-free."

"Don't underestimate yourself," Thomas smiled.

"I'm a realist, Mr. Curry. Ninety percent of the time, unless a killer is seen in the act or is caught with incriminating evidence within two hours after the crime, murders don't get solved. You know why we do all that fingerprint and ballistics stuff most of the time?"

"No."

"People expect us to. They watch Rod Taylor on 'The Detectives' or that young guy on 'Naked City' and they figure that's what cops do when they investigate a crime. So, we do that because otherwise people'll think we're not trying."

"But it doesn't solve crimes?"

"Not usually. Now, some big shots get murdered, that's different. If someone found the chairman of Chemical Bank leaning on an ice pick, I'd have as many flatfoots as I needed tracking down every ice pick sold in New York in the last six months and tracing every dollar that everyone who was in that press box spends for the next two years."

"A hustler from Hell's Kitchen doesn't rate that kind of effort, though?"

"No, he doesn't. That's just life in the big city."

"Why are you telling us all this?"

"To try to persuade you to tell me everything you know."

"You've succeeded," Thomas said. "I think you're right. I think Jerry was in the middle of something, and I think he had a role in mind for Sandy and me or at least one of us. But I don't know what he was doing, and I don't know why he wanted me or Sandy there."

"Tell me this, then," Bernstein pressed. "Why do you think I'm right? What makes you think Jerry's Polo Grounds gathering last night had some ulterior motive behind it?"

Thomas described the series of private conferences that Fielder had arranged in the press box. Then, after pausing and thinking it over for a moment, he described the conversation on September 22, when Fielder had asked him about reasonable reliance.

"See?" Bernstein said. "You know more than you thought you did."

"Now we all know it," Thomas responded.

"You know," Bernstein said then after a long pause, "if your offer of something to drink is still good, I think I'm about ready to take you up on it."

".Name it," Thomas said.

"You'd have to work very hard to find a beer I don't like."

"Coming up."

Thomas waved Sandy back to her seat and headed for the kitchen. Bernstein excused himself and followed Thomas.

Taking a bottle of Löwenbräu from the refrigerator, Thomas opened it and poured the beer down the side of a tapered stein that he pulled from the cupboard over the sink. When he had finished the head foamed a frothy inch from the top of the glass.

"The first place I looked for you and Mrs. Curry today was at your office," Bernstein said as he accepted the beer.

"Sandy's office, actually. I only work there sporadically, on an assignment-by-assignment basis."

"While I was asking after you there, the blind gentleman who runs the newspaper and tobacco stand on the first floor of the building mentioned that someone had left an envelope

84

for you. It took some doing, but I finally managed to talk him out of it."

Bernstein took a white business envelope out of the left inside pocket of his suit coat. It was slit neatly open along its top border. He handed it to Thomas.

"Was it in this condition when Fran gave it to you?"

"Exactly this condition, except that it was unopened and its contents hadn't been disturbed."

"Isn't there a rule or something against opening citizens' mail?"

"Probably," Bernstein smiled from beneath a froth-speckled moustache. "There's a rule against sticking ice picks in guys I like, too."

Thomas took a thrice-folded, slick magazine page from the envelope. Opening it, he found himself looking at a glossy, full-page, four-color drawing of a young white woman's head and upper body. She wore a straw summer hat and gloves of white cotton. She was holding in the foreground of the picture an unlighted cigarette in such a way as to emphasize its recessed filter. Prominent words above her hat read, "Parliament—Neat and Clean."

"She looks quite charming," Thomas commented, "although I suppose if she has such an aversion to tobacco she could dispense with smoking altogether."

"I think the message is on the other side."

Thomas turned the sheet over. Three columns of printing in the unmistakable *New Yorker* typeface confronted him. (That's how innocent things were in 1962—*The New Yorker* still accepted cigarette advertisements.) Some words, parts of words, and individual letters were underlined in blue ball-point pen. Thomas had to study the underlined portions for nearly a minute before he could puzzle out the intended meaning.

" 'If your still sleeping with my wife after you get this, the next time I see you will be to kill you,' " he read then. "Misspelled 'you're,' didn't he?"

Bernstein slowly swallowed a generous portion of beer. He

ran the tip of his tongue delicately along the bottom of his moustache.

"Would you like us to arrest the person who left this message for you?"

"Yes, as a matter of fact. If it's not too much trouble I'd like that very much."

"What's his name?"

"I don't have the faintest idea what his name is."

"Well," Bernstein said with elaborate patience, "how many guys' wives are you sleeping with?"

"Only one," Thomas said. He tapped his own chest and smiled a chilly, just-for-the-record smile.

"I was pretty sure that's what you'd say," Bernstein nodded. "I hope to God you're telling the truth."

"Because otherwise I'm in danger?" Thomas asked.

"No. You're in danger either way. But if you're telling the truth, this poison-pen exercise is almost certainly tied in some way to Jerry Fielder's death—which means the killer may have given us a lead we couldn't have gotten any other way."

"In that case," Thomas said, "this page may be evidence and you'll want to hang onto it. Do you mind if I show it to Sandy before you take off with it?"

"Up to you," Bernstein shrugged.

When they got back into the apartment's living room they found Sandy sitting on the couch, absorbed in *Lust for Life*, Irving Stone's popular biography of Van Gogh.

"Sorry we took so long," Thomas said. "Look at what Lieutenant Bernstein found. It's a message that someone left for me with Fran."

Sandy glanced over the page of type, apparently taking only fifteen seconds or so to grasp the thrust of the intended communication.

"My word," she said, her voice suggesting vaguely bored puzzlement. "What a great deal of trouble to go to for such a lame prank."

"Well," Bernstein said, "if you remember anything else you think I should know about, give me a call."

He put a business card on the corner of the coffee table. He retrieved the photocopy of the sign-out sheet that was still lying there and folded it back into his coat pocket. He did the same with the *New Yorker* page that Sandy returned to him.

"Good luck," Thomas said as he shook hands with Bernstein at the door.

"Yes," Sandy added. "Happy hunting."

"Thanks."

Bernstein put on his hat and left. Thomas turned back to Sandy.

"Interesting character. For a detective, I mean."

"Yes."

"Uh, Sandy," Thomas said then, "you really don't think that I've ah, uh, um—"

"—been intimate?" she suggested, her eyes laughing at his discomfiture.

"Well, yes, I suppose. I mean, with anyone other than you, of course."

"Thomas, you precious idiot." She threw her arms around him and laid her head on his chest as she laughed. "You have neither the guile for adultery in general nor the bad taste to deceive me in particular. *A mon avis* you are above suspicion."

Sandy's tone was utterly confident. Gazing anxiously at the top of his wife's head, Thomas couldn't see the flicker of uncertainty that marred her expression for an instant.

"Good," Thomas said. "Did you copy out the information from the sign-out sheet while Bernstein and I were in the kitchen?"

"*Mais bien sûr*. It is on the end pages of the book I was pretending to read."

Chapter
Twelve

"I remember Jerry Fielder vaguely, and his wife only a little better," T. Graham Curry said. "Detective Lieutenant Herschel Bernstein, on the other hand, I shall never forget."

"How do you know Bernstein?" I asked.

"I had to cross-examine him in a murder case in 'fifty-six or 'fifty-seven. The whole case stood or fell on two witnesses, and he was one of them. I learned everything I could about him. A lot of it stayed with me."

"Was your cross-examination successful?" Sandy asked.

"My client will be eligible for parole in 1975. I regard it as a moral victory."

It was about six-fifteen on the evening of September 27. Four of us—T. Graham, Thomas, Sandy and I—were sitting in T. Graham's office, discussing Bernstein's remarkable interview that afternoon with Thomas and Sandy.

"What did you find so interesting about Bernstein?" Thomas asked his father.

"He's an unusual kind of cop. He trained himself to be a bookkeeper. He studied it during minutes he could steal away from helping out in the family deli over in the Bronx. Took the competitive civil service examinations at every New York City agency in the mid-thirties. The only nibble he got was from the NYPD—and it was an offer to be a cop, not a bean-counter."

"A policeman in spite of himself," I commented.

"A good one though," T. Graham affirmed. "He made detective during the war and was assigned to homicide by the mid-forties. Eight men that he arrested have gone to the electric chair."

"A notch-cutter," Thomas said.

"Excuse me?" Sandy asked.

"Like the gunfighters in the old West who cut notches on their guns every time they killed a man. We had a guy like that when I was at the U.S. Attorney's office. He kept track of the sentences given to everyone he prosecuted. When he finally got to ten thousand years he brought a magnum of champagne in and treated the entire staff."

"What egregiously bad taste," I commented.

"That would depend on whether the champagne was domestic or imported, no?" Sandy remarked.

"Bernstein wasn't in that category at all," T. Graham said brusquely. "He knew the life histories of each of those eight men. They were flesh-and-blood human beings to him, not tally marks in a personal copybook."

"Do you suppose he lost any sleep over the electrocutions?" Thomas asked skeptically.

"I doubt it very much. The executions didn't bother him, but I don't think they were a source of pride or satisfaction, either. He seemed to view the process as some kind of force of nature: Killers kill, cops catch them, and society puts them to death the same way cats catch mice and dogs chase cats."

"What a loss to American accounting when he picked up a

billy club," Thomas said. "Imagine what fun he might have had with a full-scale audit."

"It's a matter of taste, I suppose," T. Graham replied, "but I rather like my cops that way. As a general proposition I like for people who carry guns to acquire the habit of doing what they're told."

"*Bien*," Sandy said. "But you said that he was very good at being a policeman. So he must be able to think for himself to some extent, must he not?"

"He certainly can," T. Graham agreed. "He may not know Remington from Bingham, but he's smart and shrewd and he knows how to get what he wants."

"So shrewd that he absentmindedly left a key piece of physical evidence lying around where Sandy could copy it while he was chewing the fat with Thomas in the next room?" I asked.

"I've been thinking about that," T. Graham nodded. "I can't help wondering if that was quite as absentminded as it appeared."

"What are you suggesting?" Thomas asked.

"That perhaps he wanted you to copy the information on that sheet."

"Instead of us outsmarting him he was manipulating us?" Sandy mused.

"It's happened to people savvier and more experienced than you," T. Graham said.

"Who?"

"Me."

"But why?" Thomas wondered out loud. "Inviting us to inject ourselves into his investigation is exactly the opposite of what you'd expect him to do."

"That would depend on whether he's more interested in credit or results, wouldn't it?"

"What do you mean?"

"He told you four key things. One: This isn't just another murder investigation. Jerry Fielder was someone he liked and he wants the killer caught."

"Correct," Sandy said.

"Two: The starting point is the sign-out sheet, which he allowed you to copy."

"Right," Thomas said.

"Three: Someone sent a threatening message to Thomas under circumstances suggesting the possibility of a connection with Fielder's murder."

"Okay. And four?"

"And four: The resources the police can devote to a case like this are limited and probably insufficient for the task."

"And you think the point of all that was to make us jump into this mess ourselves?" Thomas asked.

"A plausible hypothesis," Sandy said. "After all, that is precisely the effect that it had."

"I thought as much," T. Graham said. "Where do you plan to start?"

"Mary Margaret Fielder and R.J. Madden, I suppose," Thomas said.

"If there's anything I can do to help, please let me know. Meanwhile, I do have one suggestion based on the, ah, brief but intense contacts I had with Mrs. Fielder while I was representing her husband."

"And what suggestion is that?" Sandy asked, amused at the delicate verbal waltz T. Graham was dancing with his son.

"It may be best if Sandy talked to Mrs. Fielder alone. Mrs. Fielder is very, uh, Irish."

"She can hardly help that, can she?" Thomas asked.

"Her racial resentment of Anglo-Saxons and all their works is quite catholic—small c," T. Graham added with a hasty glance at Sandy. "She doesn't discriminate in this ill feeling between those technically English and their American cousins from bluestocking, Ivy League backgrounds. When I was dealing with her, she made it clear that she disliked me in a quite personal way because she still hadn't forgiven the British for suppressing the Easter Rebellion in 1916."

"In that case we should get along famously," Sandy said.

"I still haven't forgiven them for burning Joan of Arc in 1431."

And so the cards were on the table. Well, part of the cards. I realized, if Thomas and Sandy didn't, that despite the detachment he affected T. Graham hadn't actually promised to limit his own involvement in this little enterprise to occasional pieces of sage advice. I decided to keep this insight to myself.

As the meeting broke up and Thomas and Sandy prepared to leave, T. Graham leaned drowsily back in his chair and offered one last comment.

"By the way," he said, "please do bear in mind as you proceed that the line between aggressive volunteerism and officious intermeddling is notoriously indistinct. Obstruction of justice or suppression of evidence would be a crime."

"If half of what you say about Detective Lieutenant Bernstein is true," Sandy said, "it would be worse than that. It would be a mistake."

September 28

200 POLICEMEN WITH CLUBS RING
CAMPUS TO BAR NEGRO
New York Times, September 28, 1962, p. 1, col. 6

MOSCOW RIDICULES U.S. ON CUBAN
PORT
New York Times, September 28, 1962, p. 1, col. 1

TAKE A PUFF—IT'S SPRINGTIME!
Television commercial for Salem cigarettes

Chapter Thirteen

"Someone's here, Mom," the boy called over his shoulder.

He looked about twelve. His vivid red hair was cut as close to his head as it could have been without actually taking it off at the scalp. He was wearing his parochial school uniform—long-sleeved white dress shirt, navy blue tie and slacks—and he clearly felt uncomfortable wearing this outfit on a day he hadn't gone to school.

"Find out who it is and what he wants," Mary Margaret Fielder's voice yelled from deeper inside the fourth floor apartment.

"I am Sandrine Curry," Sandy said before the twelve-year-old could relay the question. "I wish to speak with your mother for a moment."

"Okay," he shrugged. "Come on in, I guess."

A cooked vegetable smell permeated the modest-sized,

overfurnished room that Sandy stepped into. A tan couch and matching wing chairs framed a wooden coffee table to her left. Transparent, plastic covers were zippered over the cushions on the couch and the chairs. An oval, ribbed area rug done in chocolate brown and mustard yellow covered about three-quarters of the floor. A television in an enormous wooden cabinet sat opposite the couch and chairs. The room was spotless.

Mary Margaret Fielder scurried into view, looking harried. She held a dust rag in one hand and a can of Pledge in the other. A scarf held her hair back from her forehead.

"I don't have time—Oh, hi. You were one of the ones at the game night before last, weren't you?"

"Yes. I was there with my husband, Thomas. I wanted to come by to say how sorry Thomas and I are about your misfortune."

"Thanks. Michael, go help Bridget in the bedroom." The boy disappeared down a hallway.

"I also wished to bring this by and leave it with you, if you have any use for it."

Sandy held out a mayonnaise jar half full of brownish red liquid, and a rectangular aluminum cooking pan covered with Reynolds Wrap.

"Beef brisket," Sandy said. "It is one of Thomas's favorite recipes. It has already been cooked except for the last hour. An hour before you are ready to serve it if you will score it, pour the sauce over it, and roast it for sixty minutes at two hundred degrees, it should be ideal."

"God bless you," Mary Margaret said fervently. "This'll be perfect for tomorrow. You've saved me two hours."

"Let me take it to the kitchen for you," Sandy said. "Your hands are full and I can see you are busy enough."

"You're a saint."

"I am afraid not," Sandy answered as she followed Mary Margaret around a corner, past a dining table and into a minuscule kitchen, "but I know that this must be a difficult time for you." A girl who looked a year or so older than

Michael was slicing tomatoes on the counter next to the sink.

"That it is." Mary Margaret took the food Sandy had brought, opened a white, round-topped refrigerator by hooking the latch with her elbow, and deftly found a place on the crowded shelves for the new items. "Listen. I wish I could thank you properly without seeming to be in a rush and everything, but I have the wake tomorrow and a meal for everybody here and then the funeral on Monday and another meal that afternoon."

"I understand perfectly. Is there anything I can do?"

"Oh, listen, I couldn't—"

The girl slicing the tomatoes interrupted this disclaimer. She had just produced a slice that looked like a misshapen polygon and on her next attempted cut had flattened the tomato into a gooey residue of juice, pulp, and seeds. She muttered something under her breath.

"What was that, Colleen?" Mary Margaret demanded.

" 'Heaven preserve us,' " the girl said, choosing an ejaculation that left the Second Commandment unviolated. "Ouch!" she protested then as the palm of Mary Margaret's right hand vigorously smacked the seat of Colleen's skirt.

"That was in case it was something else," Mary Margaret explained.

"What if it wasn't?" Colleen asked crossly.

"Then offer it up. And if you'd like another one to offer up along with it, just talk back one more time."

Colleen, prudently silent, suggested defiance only by slamming the next tomato onto the counter considerably harder than she had to.

"May I attempt that?" Sandy asked quietly. "I feel quite useless just standing here."

Mary Margaret glanced appraisingly from her angry daughter to Sandy. She didn't look happy at the prospect of incorporating irregular polygons instead of tomato wedges into the tossed salad being prepared for the next day.

"Listen, Colleen," she said. "We'll take care of the tomatoes. You run down to the parish center with Michael and see if we can borrow eight or ten folding chairs until Tuesday."

Colleen exited promptly and with undisguised enthusiasm.

Sandy rolled her sleeves up and examined the knife Colleen had been using. Mary Margaret cleared away the mess her daughter had made of the vegetables she'd attacked so far.

"Do you have a hone?" Sandy asked.

Mary Margaret took a dark stone block from a drawer and put it in front of Sandy. Sandy began to draw the knife blade across one edge of the block, slowly at first and then with faster and shorter strokes.

"I'm pretty sure you weren't one of his girlfriends," Mary Margaret said, her voice quiet and matter-of-fact.

"No, I wasn't."

Sandy glanced at the refrigerator, where Scotch tape held one of Michael's spelling tests to the door, displaying the perfect score he'd gotten. "A.M.D.G." was written carefully in the upper right-hand corner.

"*Ad majorem Dei gloriam,*" Sandy said then. "I used to write the same initials on my school papers in France."

"I thought you might be Catholic," Mary Margaret nodded. "But that's not why I figured you weren't one of his girlfriends. If all the Catholic girls Jerry slept with end up in Hell there'll be enough of them to form their own Altar Society."

"Well, however you arrived at it, your conclusion is correct."

"It's just a feeling you have, you know?"

"Yes, I do know."

"You're pretty enough in your way but you're not Jerry's type. He liked girls with bigger breasts and not quite as cocksure as you are."

Blue sparks flew from the sharpening block. Sandy closed her eyes and smiled briefly.

"Thank you, I think," she said, unconsciously lapsing into a locution she'd picked up from Thomas.

Sandy held the knife up and examined it critically. Putting the hone aside, she placed a whole tomato in front of her and sliced it effortlessly in half. She then halved each of the halves, then each of the quarters. She used the knife blade to push the eight wedges toward the edge of the counter and reached for another tomato. The entire operation had taken about five seconds.

"You're pretty good at that, you know that?" Mary Margaret said. She made this comment as she took a large, plastic dry-cleaning bag out from under the sink and shook it open.

"Thank you."

Sixteen tomato wedges now lay at the end of the counter. Mary Margaret took three heads of lettuce from the refrigerator, washed them, and began throwing damp green leaves into the dry-cleaning bag.

"I hope I didn't rub you the wrong way with that girlfriend crack," she said to Sandy.

"Not at all. You'd only seen me once in your life, and you are wondering why I had such an interest in Jerry that I came over here today."

"That's exactly right." Mary Margaret began dropping tomato wedges into the dry-cleaning bag.

"Jerry was a friend of mine and of Thomas."

"Jerry was friends with a lot of people."

"And enemies with at least one, it appears."

"It looks that way, doesn't it? Why don't you try that knife on some radishes?"

Sandy glanced at Mary Margaret as the older woman fetched a dozen radishes from the refrigerator and ran them under tap water.

"I suppose I ought to be choking back tears and dabbing my eyes," Mary Margaret said. "I'm just not that way, is part of it. Plus, I guess I feel it was better for Jerry to go this way."

" 'Better'?"

"I don't mean now, but all at once, in the middle of something."

"I do not understand you."

"Jerry just wasn't meant to grow up. If something like this hadn't happened sooner or later, someday he just would've had to go from schoolboy to old man overnight. It was better this way."

"You really loved him, didn't you?"

"Yeah, I did. I know I'm not talking like it, but—"

"But perhaps there is more than one way to talk about love?"

"Look. Put it this way. He never beat me. He never hit the kids unless I made him. He never gambled the table money. He never cheated on me with anyone I knew. He never got drunk more than once a week, and he put on a tie for the little ones' first communions. He was your basic C-plus as far as men are concerned."

"You said that Jerry was in the middle of something when he was murdered Wednesday night," Sandy commented. "I am sure you are right."

"Well, Jerry was usually in the middle of something."

"Thomas and I both think that Jerry had a particular reason for wanting us at the game that night. Unfortunately, we have no idea what the reason was. Do you know?"

"You're really a straight-ahead kind of girl, aren't you?"

"That has always seemed the best way to me."

"I don't know why Jerry wanted you there. If Jerry'd had his way, I would've thought that he went out to manage a gym every day. He did everything he could to keep from getting me mixed up in the shady business that he did."

Mary Margaret and Sandy between them had by now succeeded in filling the dry-cleaning bag with lettuce, tomato wedges, and sliced radishes. Mary Margaret holding the top twisted tightly shut, and Sandy holding the bottom, they shook the bag vigorously to mix the vegetables.

"Thank you," Mary Margaret said. "Again."

"You are welcome. Do you mind telling me why you and R.J. left the game early?"

"A little baseball goes a long way with me," Mary Margaret shrugged.

100

"And why did R.J. go with you?"

"From the Polo Grounds to this apartment takes you through some dangerous neighborhoods."

"Did you notice Jerry doing anything unusual in the last pair of weeks or so?"

"Everything Jerry did most of the time was unusual the way most people think of usual."

"And you have no idea at all what was going on with Jerry the night before last?"

"I just can't help you with this. Jerry's gone. Stir around in this thing and when you're all through Jerry'll still be gone."

"I appreciate the time you spent with me," Sandy said. "If there is anything further I can do to help, please let me know." She wrote her name on a Curry & Furst business card and handed it to Mary Margaret.

"Sure," Mary Margaret said. "The wake is tomorrow at McIntyre Funeral Home. It's an Irish wake: one rosary and we head back here for the food. You're welcome to come."

"Thank you," Sandy said. "Perhaps we will."

Chapter Fourteen

"**S**he didn't really learn a great deal, did she?"
T. Graham asked me.

I glanced down at the disordered pile of pleading files
cluttering the top of his massive desk. A few minutes before,
Sandy had given me the highlights of her talk with Mary
Margaret Fielder. I'd gone in to see T. Graham about something completely unrelated, and without quite knowing how
it happened, immediately found myself sharing Sandy's information with him.

"She learned that Mary Margaret loved her husband," I
shrugged. "Whether that's a great deal is a matter of opinion."

"It's something, I suppose," T. Graham allowed. "At least
Mary Margaret can come off the list of suspects."

"Not on that ground," I said. "As Sandy commented,
we're more likely to kill those we love than those we don't."

T. Graham's snow-white eyebrows arched skeptically.

"She stabs her husband through the heart and then less than two days later spanks her daughter for using a naughty word? A rather implausible combination of moral scrupulosity and ethical depravity, don't you think?"

"Not really," I demurred. "I believe it was Madame de Montespan who said that the flesh is weak and will inevitably sin, but that is no excuse for adding to the sins of the flesh those of atheism and blasphemy."

"Who's Mrs. Montespan when she's at home?" T. Graham's education had passed rather lightly over European history between 1492 and 1775.

"She was a lady of the court of Louis Quatorze. She was celebrated for the strictness of her Lenten fasts, the regularity of her attendance at mass, and the eight illegitimate children that she bore the king."

"She didn't stab anyone, I take it?" T. Graham pressed.

"The principle's the same," I assured him airily. "Historically, Catholics have killed a lot more people than they've divorced."

"Anything else Sandy picked up that she thinks is useful?"

"She's not sure. Mrs. Fielder was evasive when Sandy asked what Jerry was involved in the night he was killed, and tried to create the impression that she had no idea. Then she tried to squelch any idea of investigating his death."

"Signifying what?" T. Graham demanded."

"Perhaps nothing. Or perhaps that she knows exactly what her husband was involved in, and she fears that disclosing it would hurt her—or someone she cares about."

"So they're still really at square one," T. Graham mused. "They can't make any real progress until they figure out exactly what this Celtic hustler friend of theirs was up to."

"That's Sandy's opinion as well. When I left her she was getting ready to call R.J. to tell him that Thomas was going to try to get over to see him this afternoon."

"The French are slaves to etiquette. I can't think of any better way to guarantee that R.J. won't be within fifteen

103

blocks of the Columbus Avenue Gym when Thomas gets there."

"Would you like to tell that to her?" I asked.

"Fat chance," T. Graham snorted.

"The results of her efforts do seem a little thin so far," I conceded then.

"If they were any thinner they'd be invisible. But that's not the nub of the problem. The real difficulty is that what Thomas and Sandy are doing has no theme. An experienced detective has talked to the widow Fielder and to this prematurely faded athlete, Archie—"

"R.J."

"R.J. then, as well. Thomas and Sandy are improvising amateurs. How can they expect to learn anything the police haven't simply by talking to the same people?"

"Perhaps they have something more ambitious in mind." I offered this as a throwaway line. If only I'd known.

"Well," T. Graham said, slapping his desk with an air of finality, "perhaps so."

"You don't sound particularly convinced."

"My doubts are stronger than my hopes. But in any event I don't see what you or I can do. At the moment, at least."

"Neither do I."

"It's their case."

"It certainly is."

"If they want our help, they know how to ask for it."

"Quite right," I said.

"Which they haven't done."

"No, they haven't."

"For us to jump in without invitation would be—"

"Outrageously meddlesome."

"Exactly. Theodore, it's gratifying to see that in thirteen years as my partner you've learned something."

"Well," I said, getting out of my chair and taking a preliminary step or two toward the door, "we're agreed, then."

"Yes, we are."

I paused at the door and turned back.

104

"If I don't see you again before the end of the day, have a pleasant weekend," I said.

"Thank you. You also."

I sauntered away, the very picture of nonchalance. Not an ounce of guile in my body. On the way back to my office, I stuck my head in Ron Collins's exiguous quarters and asked, just as casually as you please, whether he could join me for a few minutes. He instantly fished a legal pad out from under the mountain of work on his desk and followed me.

"I know you're overworked," I said apologetically.

"Well—" he stammered.

"Could you possibly find time to fly to London this weekend on an emergency basis?"

"Sure," he beamed.

"Good. Then you'll have time for the much less time-consuming project I have in mind."

"What is it?" he asked resignedly, irritated with himself for walking into the oldest trap in the corporate lawyer's handbook.

"Long Island Trucking, Warehouse and Storage. Cor-Mart Appliances and Electronics. And—" I hesitated, wondering if it was worth the trouble. Then, shrugging mentally, I decided I should leave no stone unturned, especially since Collins was going to be doing the turning. "And Calliphonics Limited. I want you to go to the New York County and Long Island Unemployment Compensation offices. I want the name, address, and telephone number of everyone who lost his job with one of those companies in the last year, and whose application for unemployment compensation was opposed by the employer."

"Oh," Collins grunted, scribbling furiously as he bobbed his head, "you need a witness who knows how to hold a grudge. Got it." He scampered out of my office.

I felt guilty for about ten seconds. Then I got over it. As the Wall Street saying goes, every young lawyer should have a hobby—law.

It took me a few more minutes to understand that I'd been

had. When the realization finally hit me, I purposively re-traced my steps to T. Graham's office. As I stuck my head back in his doorway, he was just hanging up his phone.

"In thirteen years as your partner, I have learned some-thing," I said. "I just don't want you to think you're getting away with anything. I know exactly what you're up to."

"I have no idea what you're talking about, Furst," he said, the personification of cherubic innocence. Beaming, he opened a file and pretended to start reading from it. "I've just been talking to my bookie, that's all."

Chapter Fifteen

About the last thing R.J. felt like doing was shooting the breeze for forty-five minutes with Thomas Andrew Curry. So he figured that Sandy had done him a favor by calling to let him know that her husband would be dropping by that afternoon.

Laboriously, he wrote Sandy's message out on a piece of yellow scrap paper. He made sure Jerry's office—what used to be Jerry's office—was securely locked. Then he went upstairs to the Columbus Avenue Gym's courtesy counter and handed the folded paper to the elderly man behind it.

"Listen, Al," R.J. said, "I've gotta run out and take carra some things for Jerry."

"For Jerry?"

"You know. Some thingsa Jerry's for Mary Margaret and the kids."

"Sure."

"I'll be gone mosta the afternoon, maybe the resta the day."

"Sure."

"Some guy named Curry comes lookin' for me, that message's for him. It's from his wife."

"Sure."

R.J. killed most of the afternoon at a matinee showing of *McLintock,* watching John Wayne have a fistfight in a mud pit and then sort things out in no uncertain terms with Maureen O'Hara. Then he had a pastrami sandwich at Lindsay's. After the sandwich, he found a tavern and put away two boilermakers, while he watched the regulars play bar dice. That left him feeling almost confident enough to go back to the gym.

Almost but not quite. He noticed that *Donovan's Reef* was playing at Loew's, so he spent another two hours watching John Wayne have a fistfight in a Pacific island saloon and then sort things out in no uncertain terms with an actress considerably younger than Maureen O'Hara, whose name he couldn't remember ten minutes after the movie was over. By then it was pushing 10:00 and he figured it was safe to go back to the gym.

A few people were lingering around the courtesy counter when he let himself in the staff door, but the rest of the gym seemed dark. He took the shortcut through the shower room behind the basketball court, the squeak of his high-top Converses on the tile floor comfortingly familiar.

When he got to the top of the stairs leading down to the office, he heard a sound that seemed out of place. It bothered him. He stopped and listened carefully. Smack-and-smack-and-smack-and-smack. There was no mistaking the rhythmic cycle of a basketball being dribbled idly against the concrete floor outside the office downstairs.

"Who's down there?" he called. "Gym's closing. Time ta clear out."

"Is that you, R.J.?" a rather languid voice asked from the bottom of the stairs. "Come on down."

R.J. took the stairs two at a time. He looked anxiously at

the office door and saw with relief that the padlock was still in place. The unequivocal notice was still on the door:

OFFICE

PRIVATE

NO ADMITTANCE TO ANYONE

DEFENSE D'ENTRER

VERBOTEN GEKOMMIN IN

KEEP OUT

THIS MEANS YOU

It struck R.J. as reassuringly forbidding.

R.J. turned his attention to Thomas Andrew Curry, wearing a gray N.Y.U. crew-neck sweatshirt, matching baggy sweatpants, and low-cut court shoes.

"What're you doin' here?" R.J. demanded.

"Waiting for you."

Thomas smiled disarmingly and launched the basketball he was holding in a gentle pass across the twelve feet of space that separated him from R.J. The tall young man captured the ball effortlessly in his massive hands just before it would have brushed the maroon T-shirt he was wearing.

"Too much arch," he said, smiling slightly. "Ya gonna put arch on a pass ya might as well hang a little sign on the ball saying 'steal me.' Basketball passes should be in straight lines, right on the letters."

He zipped the ball hard and straight back at Thomas. It hit Thomas's sweatshirt on the N and the Y as Thomas got his hands around the ball and staggered backward a step.

"Good tip," Thomas nodded. "Worth waiting for."

"I guess that's all you're gonna get outta the wait. I'm not in the mood for a talk. Shove off."

"Oh, not bad. How've things been going with you?"

"Look, Mr. Curry," R.J. said, a charmingly bashful smile playing at his lips. "Let's just skip it, okay? I just don't feel like talkin' right now an' you don't look like you're big enough to make me. So let's just not do it an' say we did, okay?"

"Tell me something, R.J.," Thomas said. "How do you spell 'you're'? As in, 'Mr. Curry, if you don't shove off you're gonna get hurt.' "

"I stopped doing spelling tests after eighth grade, Mr. Curry. Now head 'em up and move 'em out." He jerked his left thumb toward the door.

"R.J., would you have any objection if I showed Lieutenant Bernstein this message from Sandy that you wrote out for my benefit?"

Thomas tossed up the wadded piece of scrap paper that R.J. had left for him at the courtesy counter nearly ten hours before. R.J. snatched it reflexively out of the air, unwadded it, and glanced at his own handwriting: "For Thos. Curry: Sandy says if your going to be late call."

"What's that 'spose to prove?" R.J. asked.

"You wrote 'y-o-u-r' instead of 'y-o-u-'r-e' for 'you are,' " Thomas said.

"My major at BC was geology," R.J. grinned. "Rocks for jocks. The only thing I had to be able to spell right was my name on the final exam. So I can't spell. Arrest me."

"Someone created a threatening message for me by marking up a page from this week's New Yorker. That guy had the same problem—misspelled 'you're' the same way you did."

"There must be a million guys coulda made that mistake."

"There aren't a million guys who found out in the last few days that a message would get to me if it was left at the building where my father's firm has its offices, R.J."

Silence hung in the room for several moments. R.J.'s thought process was so deliberate as to seem almost audible. He looked intently at Thomas. Beads of perspiration pearled his forehead. Then he walked over to the office door and started fussing with keys on a thong that he fished from his left pants pocket.

"Bad spellin's not a crime," he said over his shoulder, "and knowin' where your dad works is nothin' but coincidence." He inserted a key and snapped open the padlock. "Don't try to follow me in here," he said as he cracked the door. "That sign means what it says."

"No doubt."

He opened the door the rest of the way, turned his back confidently on Thomas, and stepped across the threshold of the office.

"Hello, R. J.," Sandy said from inside. "Did you know there was a page missing from the copy of *The New Yorker* magazine that is in here?"

She held up the copy in question, smiling insouciantly.

R.J. turned around and stared at Thomas, his face suddenly vacant.

"So you were just the lookout," he said. "How'd you get in?"

"R.J.," Thomas said, "there're guys hanging around this gym who could get into the vault at First National City Bank. They all liked Jerry. One of them was very cooperative and quite reasonably priced. It couldn't have been any easier if a cop they trusted had dropped the word that Sandy and I were on the side of the angels."

R.J.'s shoulders slumped. He bowed his head and, fists on his hips, examined the floor.

"Whadda you wanna know?" he sighed.

"For starters," Thomas said, "I'd like to know what that message you sent me was all about."

"Well, basically," R.J. murmured, "I had a bone to pick with you."

"What was it?"

"C'mon upstairs," R.J said. "I wanna show you something."

Chapter
Sixteen

R. J. led Thomas and Sandy upstairs to the gym's basketball court. At the top of the stairs he snapped four light switches on simultaneously with the blade of his right hand. Yellow orange light flooded permanent goals at either end of the court and two auxiliary backboards and baskets along each side.

R.J. squatted long enough to roll up the cuffs of his blue jeans and wipe his fingers on his socks. He strolled to the top of the lane underneath the nearest auxiliary basket. He nodded toward the basketball that Thomas still cradled under his arm.

"Bring it home," he said quietly.

Thomas glanced at Sandy, who shrugged with her eyebrows—a trick that only the French have mastered.

"What are you trying to prove?" Thomas called then to R.J. "You were a star on a Division I NCAA team and I was second string on an Ivy League intramural squad. Why don't we just stipulate that you can put any shot I try back in my face, and let it go at that?"

"Bring it home," R.J. repeated.

Thomas paused for a moment and then dribbled the ball deliberately to a spot about ten feet in front of R.J. He didn't press his objection any further, partly because it would've been pointless and partly because he'd grown up in New York. Just as all Englishmen think they can ride, all Irishmen think they're poets, all Frenchmen think they can seduce women, all Italians think they can sing, and all Americans think they can play poker, all male New Yorkers in 1962 thought they had a natural, inborn ability to play basketball. This utterly democratic conceit respected no lines of class, wealth, or social background. Deep in his heart, against all reason, one part of Thomas actually conjured with the possibility of showing this Boston hotshot how the game was played in the big city.

Thomas took three rhythm bounces, turned his left shoulder toward R.J., and began dribbling in his direction. Three feet from R.J. he feinted to his left, then dribbled hard four steps to his right. He turned, squared up on the basket, brought the ball over his head, jumped and shot. Effortlessly, R.J. leaped and swatted the ball out of bounds, where it smacked against the tiles on the lower part of the wall.

"You could've stuffed that right down my throat," Thomas said.

R.J. nodded.

"So what's the point?"

"What are you, six feet tall? You're not gonna shoot it over me. You hafta take it by me. Down the lane. Right down Broadway. You're lookin' for a lay-up."

Thomas retrieved the ball and returned to his starting position. He backed up almost to half court. R.J. raised his arms to about three-quarters the height of his shoulders.

Thomas took two unhurried dribbles toward the top of the key. Then he drove straight for the basket, directly at R.J., not just dribbling the ball but driving it, slamming it with emphatic smacks off the floor as his momentum built. He lowered his left shoulder. He waited for R.J. to flinch, give him the tiny crack of an opening that he'd need to get past.

R.J. didn't flinch. He didn't even flicker. He stood there like a stone wall. Six feet away. Three feet. One stride. R.J. still hadn't moved a muscle.

Thomas crashed into him full force, Thomas's left shoulder slamming into R.J.'s chest. Sweat popped from their faces. Explosive grunts from each of them merged with the dull thud of their colliding bodies.

R.J. fell directly backward. He slapped the hardwood floor with his palms as his backside landed. He managed to jerk his head up in time to keep it from hitting the floor.

Thomas sprawled a few feet away. The ball rolled along the polished hardwood. Thomas lifted his head and shook it. A throbbing ache had already begun in the back of his skull.

Bouncing to his feet, R.J. held his right hand out to Thomas.

"You surprised me," R.J. said. "You're a little bit harder than the last Princeton guy I hit."

"I guess that's something," Thomas said as he pulled himself to his feet, hurting in places he'd forgotten he had. "Now: What was the point?"

R.J.'s expression changed. His mouth became a thin, tight line and his eyes focused with a quiet intensity on Thomas.

"They said I couldn't take the charge," he said.

"Well, they were wrong. Who's 'they'?"

"The scouts, supposedly. That was the reason they gave for not drafting me."

"You didn't get drafted out of Boston College?" Thomas asked, astounded.

"Nope. I figured I'd go first round, second for sure. I didn' go at all. Didn' get a look. After the draft, I asked four teams just to come to camp and try out as a walk-on. Didn' even get an answer. I'm not saying I would've made a team. But with my shot how could I not even get drafted?"

114

"Beats me," Thomas said.

"It sure wasn' 'cause I couldn' take the charge, was it?"

"Do you have any idea what the real reason was?" Sandy asked as she joined the two men.

R.J. looked sharply toward her.

"Supposedly, there was a rumor about me, that I'd given injury reports and game plan info and that kind of inside stuff to bookmakers my senior year at BC."

"More than enough to make you poison in the NBA all right," Thomas said.

"That's the theory."

"Was the rumor true?"

"Whadda you think?"

"I'm not sure," Thomas said. "If I had to bet I'd bet no."

"You'd win."

"How did this rumor get started?"

"That's just a real good question," R.J. said. "That's the bone I had to pick with you. I kinda thought maybe you might've had somethin' to do with it."

"Me?" Thomas's voice hit the top registers of astonishment. "What in the world gave you that idea?"

"Jerry was looking into it. He'd turned up some things about you that seemed interesting."

"Like what?"

"Like you were at the U.S. Attorney's office in New York around the time I was a senior. The feds in New York are always investigating point-shaving in college basketball and sports betting and things like that."

"There is a law against it, after all," Thomas said. "And it's likely to get a bit more play on the evening news than cigarette smuggling or interstate transportation of stolen cars."

"Point is, you could've known about this rumor. And then Jerry found out that you got fired by the U.S. Attorney's office, which is the kinda thing might happen to someone who talks out of school about his work."

"I didn't get fired, I resigned."

"Why'd you leave a cushy job like that if you had any choice?"

"For good and sufficient reason."

"Plus, Jerry also found out you got disbarred a little after that. So somethin' bad musta happened."

"I didn't get disbarred. I voluntarily surrendered my license to practice law."

"There's a difference?"

"You bet."

"Anyway, Jerry thought it was fishy enough that it was worth a little closer looking into. That's why he arranged for us to run into you that first night at the Mets game."

Thomas blinked.

"And all this time I thought it was my elegant patter and irresistible good looks."

"So that's why I sent you that threat. The idea bein' that if I take you out the cops're lookin' for a jealous husband 'steada me."

"That much I'd figured out. What moved me from possible to certain on your list of suspects?"

"You're over my head."

"You said Jerry learned some things about me that made you think I might be the guy who queered your pro career by spreading a false rumor about associating with gamblers. We buddied around for three weeks or so. Then yesterday you actually took the first step in this incredibly clever plan you'd worked out to kill me. What happened to make you sure I was the one?"

"I figured that must be why Jerry had you at the game Wednesday night."

"Why did you figure that?"

"Because I couldn' see how you fit in with why he had everybody else there."

"That's also something I've been wondering about. Rather urgently wondering about, as a matter of fact. Why *did* he have everybody else there?"

R.J. hunched his shoulders and seemed to jam his head

down into them, as if bracing himself for the disbelief he expected from Thomas.

"I didn't really understand it," he said. "It was some kinda thing Jerry had goin', buyin' an' sellin' hi-fi equipment."

"Hi-fi equipment?"

"Yeah. He said he was sort of a broker, and he'd laugh when he said it, that way he used to laugh."

"Okay," Thomas nodded, "I can connect Corbett with selling hi-fi equipment. He said he owns stores that do that. And Birnham runs a truck company, so he might have something to do with delivering the stuff. But what about Kovacs? What about Liebniewicz? Where do they fit in?"

"Liebniewicz represents people who drive trucks," R.J. said.

"So? Wouldn't he be Corbett's problem rather than Jerry's?"

"You got me. I just did what I was told."

"And that still leaves Kovacs."

"Uh, Kovacs," R.J. stammered, "was, ah, someone that Jerry sometimes went to when he needed money for something."

"What does Kovacs do?"

"He's a lawyer."

"Lawyers take money away from people, they don't give money to people."

"Like I said, I just did what Jerry told me."

"What did Jerry tell you to do?"

"He had me drive him around to places he wanted to go. He had me get all these guys to come to the game Wednesday night."

"R.J., people buy and sell hi-fi equipment every day. There had to be some kind of unusual twist to what Jerry was doing to make it his kind of project."

"It started about a month ago," R.J. said, his face a study in concentration. "Basically, it was just Jerry bein' Jerry. There are only two things about it that really stuck with me."

"Tell me about them."

"Well, when we first went to Kovacs, I remember Jerry looked kinda go-ta-hell. You know, hadn' shaved in a coupla days, wearin' yesterday's shirt, that kinda thing. Not Jerry at all."

"That doesn't sound like the way you'd look if you were trying to extract money from someone."

"All I remember is, Jerry went into Kovacs's office and I sat in the waiting room just outside. I mostly couldn' hear what they said to each other. I just remember a coupla times, Jerry raised his voice. He said, 'Louie, you gotta let me have the money. I tell ya the fix is in.' "

"What fix? How much money?"

"I don't know."

"Okay." Thomas took a deep breath, pursed his lips, and blew the air out through them in discouragement. "You said there were two things about whatever this was that stuck out in your mind. What was the other one?"

"It was funny," R.J. said. "We got an order here for some hi-fi stuff, and Jerry was real put out about it."

"The Columbus Avenue Gym got a hi-fi order?"

"Well, not the gym a course," R.J. said scornfully, as if Thomas's question represented a willfully perverse interpretation of what R.J. had just said. "It was sent to J.F. Supply."

"J.F. Supply being a name Jerry used to do business under, with a mailing address here at the gym?" Thomas guessed.

"Right."

"Was this the order for the equipment that Jerry was buying and reselling?"

"No, that's just the thing. It was from some guy down in Georgia. He just wanted one outfit. It was like this little, dinky three-hundred-dollar order."

"R.J., how would someone in Georgia know about J.F. Supply?"

"From the catalog, I s'pose."

"Well, of course. From the catalog. Naturally. It would be from the catalog, wouldn't it? What catalog, R.J.?"

"Jerry had this mail-order catalog printed up. He only had

about twelve copies made, but one of 'em musta got down to this guy."

"Why would he only have a dozen copies made?"

"I don' know." Shrug.

"How did he distribute them?"

"He didn' distribute them. He just kept 'em here."

"Why would he print catalogs just to keep at the gym?"

"I don' know." Shrug.

"Why would he be upset about receiving an order?"

"You got me." Shrug. "When I brought it to him, he just looked at it and sorta tapped it and said, 'Ain't that a bitch?' "

Thomas looked at Sandy, whose face expressed bewilderment equal to his own.

"Yeah," Thomas murmured to R.J., "ain't it. Thanks for the chat, R.J. Enjoy the weekend."

"Hey," R.J. called as Thomas and Sandy walked toward the first floor exit, "aren't you gonna ask me if I still think you're the guy started the rumor?"

Thomas paused long enough to smile thinly over his shoulder.

"There's only one way you could answer that question, R.J. So I guess there's no point in asking it, is there?"

"Did he really have a chance to play professionally?" Sandy asked Thomas when they were back out on the street. "Or was he just joking with himself?"

"He had a chance all right," Thomas said. "The three-four-five rule would've guaranteed that."

"Three-four-five rule?"

"A gentlemen's agreement in the NBA, supposedly, about the maximum number of negro players a team will start: three at home, four on the road, and five in the playoffs. A tall white guy with the guts to take the charge and the touch to swish twenty-two-foot jump shots even when some other tall guy has his hand in his face has a decent shot at playing in the NBA."

"Thomas, I spent much of my childhood in French colonies, so I will not pretend to be piously shocked by racism in America. But if anyone but you were telling me this, I would think they were having a joke on me."

"It is a joke," Thomas said. "It just isn't funny."

"The disappointment must have been terrible for him," Sandy mused. "The bitterness must be eating away at him every day. But that he would actually threaten to kill someone over it seems incredible."

"Not to me," Thomas answered, shaking his head. "From the time R.J. was twelve years old and leading some south Boston parochial school to lopsided wins over public school teams, he's been liked and applauded and respected and cheered and catered to because he could play basketball. He passed his courses and got his degree without studying or doing homework because he could play basketball. If he needed money he had it. If he liked a car he got it. If he wanted a girl someone found him a girl. All because he could play basketball."

"And then, just when it was all supposed to reach its peak, it disappeared like a castle in a dream. Because of a rumor."

"The only thing the rumor affected was timing," Thomas said.

"What do you mean?"

"If he'd had a pro career, he just would've been putting the end off, not avoiding it. Maybe six years, maybe two. Sooner or later the cheering was going to stop and R.J. was going to have to adjust to life as an ordinary mortal. America isn't comfortable with its heroes after they've lost a step."

Sandy took Thomas's arm and pulled him closer.

"The Romans were kinder," she said. "They let their gladiators die in the arena, with their armor on and their swords in their hands."

September 29

MISSISSIPPI CRISIS BIG NEWS ABROAD
New York Times, September 29, 1962, p. 1, col. 7

M'NAMARA BACKS ATOMIC WEAPONS TO DEFEND BERLIN
New York Times, September 29, 1962, p. 1, col. 1

IF I'VE ONLY ONE LIFE TO LIVE, LET ME LIVE IT AS A BLONDE.
Television advertisement for Clairol hair coloring

Chapter
Seventeen

Bright and early Saturday morning I drove to Newark. Ron Collins was to blame for that. Ten months before, Ron discovered, David Mystkowiak had been fired for cause from his job as a stockboy for Calliphonics Ltd. Calliphonics had tried to block unemployment compensation for him, arguing that he'd been canned for dishonesty on the job. This was worth following up only because Collins hadn't come up with anything more promising.

It turned out that Mystkowiak no longer lived in the Brooklyn apartment listed on the unemployment compensation records and we didn't have a forwarding address. What he did have, Ron had informed me proudly, was the address of a Newark outfit called Bushido Kan Dojo.

"What's that?"

" 'School of the Way of the Warrior,' " Ron had translated. All healthy, American males had to serve two years in the armed forces back then. Ron had served his on Okinawa. "It teaches judo and karate."

"What's it have to do with Mystkowiak?"

"A week before he got fired, Mystkowiak signed a contract for a year's worth of karate lessons at Bushido Kan Dojo. He put up his 1954 green Studebaker to secure his obligations under the installment contract, and the finance company that the school discounted the contract to recorded the lien." Collins had paused, giving me time to be impressed. Then he added the clincher. "The first karate lesson tomorrow is at eight in the morning."

"Thank you, Ron. Well done."

Excess of zeal, I'd thought as I hung up. We'd better make him a partner before he gets us all in trouble. Then I resigned myself to a drive to Newark Saturday morning.

By 8:45 I was sitting in a window booth of a drugstore soda fountain across the street and down the block from Bushido Kan Dojo. I was sipping black coffee and keeping my eyes on a currency-green Studebaker parked near the judo and karate school. Just after the war, before Curry & Furst, back when I was just an insurance lawyer, I used to do this kind of thing regularly for $1200 a year.

Four or five weighty young men that I wouldn't have wanted to argue with except over the telephone spilled from the school about ten minutes later. I hustled out of the drugstore and started walking toward the Studebaker, trying as hard as I could not to look like someone with a writ of replevin and a spare set of keys.

The man who detached himself from the group and approached the driver's side door of the Studebaker appeared to be in his mid-twenties. He had wavy black hair that he wore piled high on his head. The hair was slick with Brylcreem. Brylcreem's commercials claimed that "a little dab'll do ya," but Mystkowiak wasn't taking any chances.

"Mr. Mystkowiak?" I said from about five feet away, just as he opened the door. "My name's Theodore Furst. I'm a

124

lawyer. I'd like to buy you some breakfast—and talk to you about Calliphonics Ltd."

It was depressing. Nearly twenty years as a practicing lawyer, and I couldn't come up with anything better than the absolute truth.

"What about Calliphonics?" he asked. He didn't look at me, but he stopped getting into the car.

"I think they gave you a raw deal. I'm trying to find out if they're about to do the same thing to somebody else."

Well, maybe not the *absolute* truth.

Mystkowiak relocked the car door and turned toward me. "Let's eat," he said.

The waitress came over as soon as we sat down in my booth. She and Mystkowiak greeted each other by their first names. I ordered a bagel with cream cheese and another black coffee. Mystkowiak glanced up at the waitress.

"I want a package of Hostess cream-filled cupcakes and a Coke," he said. "And I want you to give this guy here a check for a stack of buttermilk pancakes, a side of bacon, a side of link sausage, hashbrowns, and a large orange juice."

In forty-five eventful years I had by 1962 breakfasted on everything from truffles to K rations, but my stomach did flips at the thought of starting the day with chocolate-frosted devil's food cake and Coca-Cola. On the other hand, I had to admire the eccentric integrity of someone who, instead of demanding a petty bribe, would have me pay for a three-dollar breakfast, eat one costing seventeen cents, and keep the difference.

"Calliphonics said they fired you for dishonesty," I said as I went to work on the bagel. "I don't believe it. What was the real reason?"

"You know what a spiff is?" Mystkowiak asked.

I shook my head.

"It's a little bonus that a manufacturer gives for selling one of its products. Sorta like an incentive, y'know?"

I nodded.

"If there's sumpthin' they're trine, like, to push—

y'know?—they put a little card on the carton. When a sales-man sells one, he takes the card off and sends it in to the manufacturer. The manufacturer sends him back, like, seventy-five cents or sumpthin. You get the picture?"

"Sure."

"Okay. Now, when I'm at Calliphonics, I work a five-day week, Sundays and Wednesdays off and Saturdays on, okay? So that even though I work Saturdays, I get no overtime, right?"

Nod.

"All right. So the last Saturday I'm there, okay, old man Feldman tells me he's gotta put me on a split shift that day. I mean, like Saturday's yewjly a light day for me—okay?— 'cause there's almost never no deliv'ries, so I just pack up some repairs, clean the stock up a little, and listen to 'Beale Street Blues' playing through the back wall of Feldman's of-fice, okay?"

Nod.

"Right. So old man Feldman's tellin' me to take off at noon and come back at four and plan on puttin' in like four or five more hours then. Which duddn' make sense, okay, because the place closes at five on Saturdays. So that I get my eight in but it takes me till maybe nine o'clock at night to do it, and not a tenth of an hour at time-an-a-half. I mean that's how cheap the old guy was, y'know?"

"Yes."

"An' what in hell am I gonna do to kill four hours on Saturday afternoon? Head back to Brooklyn just in time to turn aroun' an' come back to work?"

Understanding nod and sympathetic shrug.

"So, anyway, I do it. I blow off at noon and come back at four, okay? An' about five-t'irty, sure enough, after the store's dark and the day's take's in the safe, this semi pulls up to the dock. No one there but old man Feldman an' me. Guess which wunna us gets ta hump three hundred hi-fi systems downstairs from the dock into the stock room?"

"Three hundred?"

126

"Three hundred. I'm not kiddin'. I'd never seen so many systems in that place. Height a the Christmas season, maybe ya got eighty."

"Why so many?"

"No idea. Anyway, I hump 'em down, an' after they're all in old man Feldman signs off on the paperwork."

"So why did he fire you?"

"Okay. While I'm haulin' those babies downstairs, I notice there's a spiff card on ev'ry wunnuv 'em. So maybe while I'm findin' room for 'em and stackin' 'em up, maybe those cards disappear from a hunnert of 'em or so."

"Ah."

"I mean, it's not like it's comin' outta his hide, is it? An' whoever's gonna end up sellin' those babies, if he's workin' overtime he's gonna get paid for it even without the spiff, iddny?"

"I see your point."

"So, I show up for work bright an' early Monday morning an' I'm there just long enough to see that those three hundred hi-fi outfits've all gone before old man Feldman shitcans me."

"They were gone?"

"That's what I said, okay?"

"Any idea what happened to them?"

"Nope. Only that whoever made it happen got double time, 'cause it hadda be on Sunday, right, an' it waddn' me, okay?"

Okay.

Everything was going according to plan. I'd let him tell his story, get it off his chest, remind himself how much he hated Calliphonics and its owner. That's the first step with a malcontent ex-employee witness. Now I had to use the opening to get some dirt on Calliphonics—something juicy that I could use to pry information out of Feldman. I smiled inwardly at my finesse.

"How long were you at Calliphonics altogether?"

"Just unner t'ree years."

"Tell me something. You ever see anything while you were

there that made you think something shady might be going on?"

"Like what?"

I shrugged in an effort to suggest that the nonanswer I was about to give was the result of coy discretion rather than complete ignorance. "Kickbacks," I said. "Payoffs to union organizers. Shading his withholding records. That kind of thing."

Mystkowiak shook his head emphatically.

"I never saw nothin' like that. Feldman was cheap, but he waddn' crooked, as far as I know. Didn' havta be. He was the authorized dealer for like ten top lines, okay? That's just, like, a license to print money, y'know?"

There were a few moments of silence while I reflected on the educational benefits of running full speed into a stone wall. There wasn't the slightest doubt in my mind that Myst-kowiak was telling the truth, and I was morally certain that if there had been anything underhanded going on at Calliphon-ics Mystkowiak would've been shrewd enough to sense it.

I put ten dollars on the table, thanked Mystkowiak for his time, and went outside to find my sensible, conservative, two-year-old Oldsmobile. Lots of creativity. Plenty of finesse. Good plan, good execution. But nothing to show for it.

It wasn't until I had three miles of highway in between me and Newark and had begun letting my mind go idly over what Thomas had told me about the case so far that I under-stood what a fatuous blockhead I'd been. It was a comforting reflection. I decided to stop in downtown Manhattan before I headed home to Long Island.

What are you doing, Theodore? I asked myself then. You're not an insurance lawyer with the ink still wet on his LL.B. any more. You're a transactional lawyer, a lawyer of wain-scotted suites and mahogany conference rooms. You don't have to worry about street law, hunting up low-rent wit-nesses and taking statements. You spend your time putting together seven-figure loans. What are you doing?

I'm having the time of my life, that's what.

128

Chapter
Eighteen

"Excuse me, but are you looking for me by any chance?"

Harry Liebniewicz, who along with his foul-tempered young companion Tony was just about to enter the building that housed Curry & Furst's offices, turned toward the limousine at the curb from which this unexpected question had come. He saw a round-faced, white-haired man leaning out the limo's rear window. The man was wearing a formal white, pleated-front shirt and a black tuxedo jacket with silk-faced lapels. He had loosened his hand-tied bow tie and unfastened the onyx collar stud at his throat.

"Ice Capades must be in town," Tony muttered.

"I guess I am looking for you," Liebniewicz said in answer to the question from the limousine. "If you're not T. Graham Curry then you're doing one helluva damned good impersonation of him."

"That's who I am. I'll have to reprimand my secretary. I don't recall having any appointments this morning."

"Appointments. That's a good one, Mr. L.," Tony said.

"I don't usually fool around too much with appointments," Liebniewicz said. "I took a chance that I could drop by and you'd be able to find about twenty minutes to talk to me. Sort of on a client relations basis. You going up to the office?"

"Not for a couple of hours or so, I'm afraid," T. Graham answered. He said it almost apologetically. Saturday morning work was standard procedure for serious New York law offices in 1962, just as it is today. "I have to see a young lady home, and then I'm planning to visit a colleague in Brooklyn."

"That's very disappointing," Liebniewicz said.

"In the interest of client relations, of course, you're more than welcome to ride along. We can have our talk and then I can arrange to have you dropped off back here or anywhere else in Manhattan you'd like."

"Is this guy for real?" Tony demanded.

"You talked me into it," Liebniewicz said.

"Of course," T. Graham added, "I'm afraid there's only room for one more back here. Are you sure your colleague won't mind waiting for you?"

"Hey, just a minute," Tony protested. "Hey, Mr. L, you really know this guy?"

The silk-stocking accent dropped from T. Graham's voice. He reverted to the Criminal Courts Building tone he used when no jurors were around.

"Back off, junior," he instructed Tony sharply. "I was springing Teamsters from jail before you were toilet-trained."

"It's okay, Tony," Liebniewicz said. "I think I can handle anything that might come up."

Liebniewicz climbed into the car and perched on the jump seat facing T. Graham and his companion. The companion had curly blond hair, the long, muscular legs of a professional dancer, and an expression of blasé world-weariness that you'd expect on a twenty-four-year-old gutting her way through a hangover.

"Anna," T. Graham said, "this gentleman, whose name I'd have to guess at—"

"Harry Liebniewicz," Liebniewicz said.

"—is a representative of the Teamsters organization, about which you may have heard from time to time. Mr. Liebniewicz, this is Miss Anna Purna, who is appearing in *I Can Get It For You Wholesale.*"

"Anna Purna?"

"My first agent had a thing about mountain climbing and a strange sense of humor," the young woman said. "You have to admit, though, it's a name that people remember."

"Pleased to meet you."

"Likewise."

Even on a Saturday morning, it took the better part of fifteen minutes to reach the apartment building in the low nineties on Broadway where Miss Purna lived. When they got there, T. Graham gallantly climbed out of the car to hold the door open for her, and then watched appreciatively as she sauntered with immense dignity past the smirking building superintendent and into the foyer.

"Nice girl," Liebniewicz commented as T. Graham slipped back into the car.

"They almost always are," T. Graham said. "Remarkably athletic, and not the least bit shy."

"Must be wonderful."

"It is. Now. What have you come to tell me about the Fielder case, which I take it is the subject of this sudden visit?"

Liebniewicz glanced to his right and spent a moment watching Riverside Drive speed by.

"What's your interest in that case?" he asked then.

"None whatever. My only interest is in my son and daughter-in-law."

"Did you know they went to see R.J. Madden last night?"

"The news doesn't come as a complete surprise," T. Graham said.

"Whadda you suppose they're trying to prove?"

"I rather think they're trying to find out who killed a friend of theirs on a night when he expected them to be with him."

"Do they know what they might be gettin' into?"

"No, they don't," T. Graham said steadily. "Neither do I, altogether, although I have somewhat more of an inkling than they do. Why don't you tell me: What exactly are they getting into?"

Liebniewicz shook his head several times.

"Does Fielder look like a Teamster hit to you?" he asked.

"No. If it had been a Teamster hit, no identifiable teamsters would've been within three miles of the Polo Grounds when it happened, and you personally would have been shaking hands with Mayor Wagner at Gracie Mansion in front of twenty witnesses at the precise moment the ice pick entered Fielder's heart."

"You have been representing Teamsters a long time, haven't you?" Liebniewicz grinned.

"Long enough."

"Do you think they're going to accomplish anything the police can't?"

"That's a harder question. Six months ago I would certainly have said no. After watching them in action together, though, I've concluded that they're rather more formidable as a team than either of them could be individually."

"Well, if your kid and his bride keep going at things the way they did with Madden last night, they might stir up some other people who're pretty formidable themselves."

"It wouldn't be the first time. They're children of this godforsaken century we've willed ourselves. They've had people mad at them with guns in their hands, as the saying goes."

"How often do you get a Teamster case these days?" Liebniewicz asked abruptly.

"Not as often as in the old days. Say one a year or so."

"What's your retainer from us?"

"I don't accept retainers."

"First lawyer I ever heard say that."

"Don't misunderstand. When I take a case I insist that the defendant pay me before I do any work. The defendant. My client. Not my client's employer."

"That's not a retainer?"

"That's a fee. It's paid before I do any work—not before the government's accused anyone of a crime in the first place, just so I'll be available on the off chance an accusation is made."

"Sounds like a pretty theoretical distinction."

"It's the difference between a criminal lawyer and a mouth-piece."

"Can't be bought, huh?" Liebniewicz grinned skeptically.

"I don't know," T. Graham said. "All I can say is that no one so far has come up with my price."

"It doesn't look like I'm going to, that's for sure."

"It doesn't make any difference. If I tried to talk Thomas into dropping this Fielder business, I'd only double his persistence."

"Maybe," Liebniewicz said. "I guess that leaves the question of whether you're going to help him or just wish him luck and see what he can do on his own."

T. Graham leaned back against the soft leather of his seat. He closed his eyes. His face took on a dreamy expression.

"Harry Liebniewicz," he said. "I didn't even know your name for certain. I just assumed you'd be the likeliest one to bring the message I was about due to get from the Teamsters. But I could write your biography without leaving many blanks. Detroit, right?"

"Yep."

"First plant gate brawl before you were twenty."

"I was fifteen. Gate three, Ford Main. Pinkertons outnumbered us three to one and I've got the scars to prove it. If every guy who said he was with Walter Reuther that day'd really been there, we'd've walked in and organized Ford right then and there. By the time I was sixteen I knew how to operate a drill press, a drop forge and a thirty-eight. That was life in thirties Detroit. It wasn't about manifest destiny and amber waves of grain. It was about blood and sweat and cold rolled steel."

"So," T. Graham said, "you're the last person I should have to explain this to."

"Huh?"

"Jerry Fielder was a friend of Thomas. He was a friend of Sandy. He made a particular point of having them with him in the press box at the Polo Grounds Wednesday night. All of a sudden they weren't there and all of a sudden Jerry Fielder passed away. Do you really think they're just going to send a wreath to the funeral, have an extra cocktail, and start looking forward to the next opening night?"

"Maybe not," Liebniewicz conceded.

"There's only one way to work it, I'm afraid," T. Graham said.

"Ice the guy who did it, huh?"

"Mr. Liebniewicz, I didn't get to be rich and famous by advising my clients to commit felonies. Tell me who it is. Let me worry about focusing the investigation on him and keeping it out of, er, meretricious channels."

"I'd tell you if I knew."

"If you knew or if you could?"

"Take it any way you like."

"Then what can you tell me? Anything?"

"All right," Liebniewicz said decisively, as if with an effort of will. "Okay. Jerry had somethin' goin'."

"What?"

"Doesn't matter. Point is, there was somethin' in it for everybody. Everybody who was in on it, that is."

"Wednesday night was payday?"

"Bingo."

"Well, it's quite simple then," T. Graham said. "Who got shorted?"

"Far as I know, no one. My share was there, just like Jerry

134

promised. If anyone got cut out, he did a great job of acting that night. Birnham looked happy enough to me and so did Corbett."

"What about Madden?"

"He always looked happy. Dumb goddamn mick."

"And Kovacs?"

"Kovacs wasn't in it that I know of."

"What was he doing there?"

"I understand Jerry tried to get some money from him."

"I understand the same thing," T. Graham said. "I also understand that he didn't get any."

"Maybe not the first time he asked."

"You're guessing?"

"True."

"Where else could he have gotten the money?"

"I don't know," Liebniewicz said. "The way he explained the deal to me, I don't know why he would've needed any money of his own. Jerry's idea of a deal was something where he didn't have his own money in it. How Jerry saw things, money came to him, not from him."

"Up front?"

"Up front, in the middle, and at the end."

"Did he get any from you? Up front, I mean?"

"Not directly."

"Ah," T. Graham said. "Now we're getting somewhere. What did he get from you indirectly?"

"A bet. Jerry said the entry fee into the deal was to bet a hundred bucks with four bookies Jerry named."

"Anything in particular you were supposed to bet on?"

"Pure Jerry," Liebniewicz smiled. "We were supposed to bet that the Mets wouldn't set a new major league record for losses in one season."

"An imprudent wager."

"Especially in September, when we had to make it. The odds were definitely the other way—an' the other way's the way it came out."

"It seems like a very odd way to do things."

"It was a small price to pay," Liebniewicz assured T. Graham. "I didn't ask any questions."

The limousine had been stopped for some five minutes on Court Street in Brooklyn. T. Graham nodded at the last piece of information he had gotten, lurched forward, and lumbered out of the car.

"Please take Mr. Liebniewicz anywhere he'd like to go," T. Graham told the driver, "and pick me up back here in ninety minutes."

The car purred away from the curb, evoking giggles and chatter from the gaggle of children romping in the block-square park on the other side of the sidewalk.

"What's the matter with you?" T. Graham muttered genially. "Haven't you ever seen a slightly hungover sexagenarian standing on the sidewalk in evening clothes at nine forty-five in the morning before?"

He glanced up and down the block opposite. The buildings were three to six stories high. Retail stores, barber shops and beauty parlors filled the first floors. On the floors above were purveyors of key services to the working class: dentists, bail bondsmen, finance companies ("Payday Loan? Grab That Phone!"), divorce and DWI lawyers, tax preparers, and so forth. On the second floor of the corner building nearest him, T. Graham saw lettered on a frosted glass window:

LOUIS J. KOVACS, ESQ.
ATTORNEY AND COUNSELLOR AT LAW
REAL AND PERSONAL PROPERTY APPRAISALS
NOTARY PUBLIC

T. Graham read the lettering with the informed eye of a native New Yorker. It told him what Kovacs did for a living: He was a bookie.

Chapter Nineteen

L et the record show that I did try to call Thomas before I went to see Feldman. So what happened wasn't really my fault.

I was back in Manhattan shortly after 9:30. (The speed limit on the New Jersey Turnpike in 1962 was seventy miles an hour. I kept it at seventy-four all the way, and most cars passed me as if I were standing still.) After parking in a lot less than a block from Park and Thirty-fifth, I closed myself into a phone booth, called the office, and asked for Thomas and Sandy.

Mrs. Walbach informed me crisply that I'd just missed them. She said they'd come in around 9:00, asked where T. Graham and I were, and then left to get ready for the Fielder wake.

I thanked her and tried the number for their apartment.

There wasn't any answer. I shrugged, reclaimed my dime, and walked up the street to Calliphonics Ltd.

A sweet, rich wood smell reached me as I stepped through the door. Strolling casually across the thick carpet, I glanced at a bulky console in a polished, maple cabinet: AM/FM radio, turntable, amplifier, two built-in speakers, shelf space for LPs (as they were called back then), and knobs to adjust balance, bass, and treble. It looked as if it weighed half a ton.

A thin, sallow-faced young man with a sepulchral voice padded up and asked if he could help me.

"I'm looking for the Johnny Maddox album by Dot that includes 'Beale Street Blues,' " I said.

"Ah, we don't actually carry LPs as such, sir," he explained. "Just a few demonstrators and test albums."

I nodded and handed him my card.

"A gentleman named Mystkowiak suggested that I might be able to pick that particular album up from Mr. Feldman personally. I'd appreciate it if you'd pass that on to him and find out whether he could see me for a few minutes."

The young man looked dubious. He smiled nervously. He thought better of the smile, took my card, and shuffled away. He was back in less than a minute to show me into Feldman's office.

Feldman sat behind a rosewood desk. He was wearing a dove gray three-piece suit and polishing his black, tortoise-shell glasses. A curved-stem briar pipe rested in a large ashtray near the front of the desk. Feldman looked as if he were going to start playing with the pipe as soon as he was through fiddling with the glasses.

He had furnished the office in an unostentatiously tasteful way: muted blue gray carpet, cream-painted walls, dark wood bookcases, leather-upholstered chairs. Something nineteenth century—Debussy, I think—played in the background.

"How is Mystkowiak doing?" Feldman asked in a distinctly unworried voice after I'd found a seat.

"As well as he'll probably ever do. They haven't repossessed his car yet."

Feldman nodded. He put on his glasses and reached for the pipe.

"How much did he tell you?"

"Enough to make me want to ask you a question."

"Shoot."

"Why did you get in bed with a cheap lowballer like Corbett?"

Feldman began to probe the bowl of the pipe with a metal pipe-cleaning tool. He smiled at me.

"You're bluffing," he said.

"I'm surmising."

"Same thing."

"I haven't heard you tell me I'm wrong yet. Knowing I'd seen Mystkowiak worried you enough to get me in here."

"I'm trying to draw you out," Feldman said. "I need to learn how much misinformation whichever of my suppliers you're representing has picked up, so that I can straighten his sales manager out at the next audio show. Which one of them are you representing, by the way?"

"None of them."

"You don't expect me to believe that, do you?"

"Suit yourself."

"Okay," Feldman shrugged. "You tracked down a malcontent with an axe to grind and the IQ of a houseplant. Did he give you anything solid or did he just tell you what a bad guy I am?"

"He told me about the three hundred outfits that were in and out of here in one weekend."

"Three hundred, huh? Pretty impressive. Is that the story he's peddling now to explain why he got fired?"

"It's a pretty convincing story the way he tells it."

"Bosh. Why would I bother to run the outfits through here if I were bootlegging to Corbett? Why not just ship them directly to him?"

"That was what had me stumped," I admitted. "Then I

started to think about how I'd put a deal like that together."

"If you figure it out, tell me. I'd really like to know."

"Three hundred outfits would cost in the low six figures anyway, and that has to be way over your credit limit with one supplier. So you must've offered some gilt-edged, iron-clad security for the deal."

"And how did I do that?"

"Irrevocable letter of credit. It wouldn't make sense to put up cash, and there's no other way a European manufacturer would take a risk like that. Europeans break out in a cold sweat just thinking about American courts."

"Letter of credit, huh? And how did I get my bank to issue one of those?"

"By posting a back-to-back letter of credit from your buyer, Corbett, who has a huge cash flow and all the credit he needs."

"What hat did you pull that particular rabbit out of?"

"That's the answer to your question. That was why the outfits had to go in and out of here in one weekend on short notice."

"What would a pile of make-work like that have to do with back-to-back irrevocable letters of credit?"

"There was a foul-up in the documentation. There had to be. That's the problem with letters of credit. Every i has to be dotted, and every t has to be crossed. If one invoice number was off or one packing slip was messed up the trucker wouldn't release the goods to Corbett. They couldn't sit in the trucks overnight, so they had to come here until Corbett could get his paperwork straightened out."

"You aren't bluffing, Mr. Furst. You don't know enough to bluff. You're guessing."

"Was Jerry Fielder guessing when he warned you not to HK Thomas Andrew Curry?" I asked.

He lost the patronizing smile for a second or so. It was the first time in the conversation that I thought I might actually be reaching him.

"Thomas didn't know what HK meant, but I do," I con-

140

tinued. "H and K are the sixth and fifth letters in 'Black Horse.' HK is retail code for a sixty-five-percent markup. Fielder was telling you that if you tried to stick Thomas with an inflated price he'd let Thomas know that he could get the same goods from a Corbett discount store."

"I see," Feldman said. "That crack ties me to Fielder, Fielder ties me to Corbett, Mystkowiak ties me to discounter bootlegging and you just put it all together."

"Easy when you know how."

"Who do you think you're kidding?"

"No one."

"You've got nothing. You're going through the motions. I deny bootlegging to anyone. Put that in your report. Your client can send me a stuffy letter, I'll send your client an indignant response, and business will go on as usual."

"Going through the motions?" I asked.

"You make me tired, Mr. Furst. A few dealers squeak about price-cutters. They don't know how to sell so they whine instead. Now you've done some legwork and tracked down some leads so whoever's paying you can tell the whiners everything possible's being done. Your supplier has a letter of credit in his files documenting a sale to Calliphonics, a duly authorized retail distributor. He can show that to the whiners. That's all he really cares about and we both know it."

And then, just like a house falling on me, I remembered Jerry's question to Thomas about reasonable reliance and fraud.

"The denial's just for the record," I said, as much to myself as to him. "That's what you're telling me. Off the record, everyone knows and they only pretend to care."

"No comment," Feldman said.

"Of course the suppliers would have to know, wouldn't they? They knew you weren't going to sell three hundred outfits at full retail. They had to know something was up."

"You're playing dumb on me now, Mr. Furst?"

"It's not an act," I said, grinning in self-deprecation as the

141

obvious finally occurred to me. "If the manufacturers suddenly find themselves with a glut, they have to find a way to cut the price and move it without any of their legitimate authorized retail distributors knowing. So they sell to you, knowing you'll bootleg to a discounter, and then they look the other way. They're in it up to their eyebrows with you, but selling to the discounter can't get pinned on them."

"You keep saying 'they' like you think you're fooling someone."

"You're being too clever for your own good, Mr. Feldman. I've already told you I'm not working for any of your suppliers."

"Then who are you working for?"

"That's a rather delicate question," I said. "Let's say I'm counsel to the situation."

"Sounds like double-talk to me."

"I stole the line from Louis Brandeis. Blame him."

" 'Counsel to the situation,' " Feldman mused. "The situation being Fielder's killing?"

"That's right. If I report to anyone it won't be a general counsel in Heidelberg. It'll be a detective in New York." I paused a beat to let that sink in, then continued. "The police in this city aren't famous for finesse. If they decide this connection is worth poking into, it might get difficult for your suppliers to go on pretending that they don't know for sure what you're up to."

Feldman sat quietly for a couple of seconds. He puffed clouds of pipe smoke casually toward the ceiling.

"So you don't actually have a client in this matter," he said distantly after the pause.

"That's right."

"Would you like to have one?"

He swiveled suddenly in his chair and looked hard at me. I can buy you and sell you three times a week, the look said.

"Yes," I said. "On two conditions."

"What are they?"

142

"First, Thomas and Sandy Curry come first. If your inter-
ests conflict with theirs, I go with them and not you."

"All right."

"Second, my fee is zero. You get the attorney-client priv-
ilege. I get information. No money changes hands."

Feldman smiled around the pipe stem. The smile puffed
up his nut brown cheeks and showed all of his teeth.

"Perry Mason always takes a dollar," he said.

"Perry Mason practices in Hollywood. This is New York."

"Okay," Feldman said decisively. "You got it right. Mystkowiak was telling you the truth. I bought a carload lot of
hi-fi outfits and sold them to Corbett for cost plus ten per
cent. Eight of the ten profit points went to Fielder and he
covered all the incidental expenses. The other two went to
me, plus the prompt payment discount, plus the spiffs."

"That's why you were so upset with Mystkowiak helping
himself to the spiff cards."

"You bet."

"Why did Fielder get the lion's share of the profit?"

"One, it was his idea. Two, he had the contacts with the
truckers so that this, ah, unconventional delivery could happen without a paper trail from Corbett to the supplier and
without me getting shaken down. Three, he provided the
cover."

"What was the cover?"

"This so-called mail-order operation he had. If push came
to shove, the supplier was supposed to be able to say that it
thought the outfits were going to a mail-order house that
couldn't resell them within a three-hundred-and-fifty mile
radius of New York City."

"And then Fielder actually got a mail order from a legitimate customer," I mused, remembering what Sandy had told
me about the conversation with Madden.

"I know exactly how it happened, too," Feldman said.
"The printer kept a few extra copies and shopped them
around. Happens all the time. Jerry was beside himself.
Didn't know whether to laugh or cry. That was why he was

in here the day he made that HK crack. He had to buy a hi-fi at retail to fill that order."

"What was so unconventional about the delivery?"

"The way it was supposed to work was, the trucks pick the shipment up from the docks with papers saying take them to Calliphonics. Somewhere along the highway, they pull over, meet someone who shows them a new set of documents and signs off on the original set, and suddenly these things are going to Corbett instead. The supplier has a clean set of documents to show the whiners when they squeak, the truckers have the proper authorization to deliver, and Corbett has the outfits."

"But Corbett messed up."

"Had one whole set of invoices out of sequence. Dumb SOB."

"It's so simple," I said, shaking my head in admiration.

"Exactly. Fielder always said the only thing he didn't like about it was it was damn near honest."

"And Fielder never had to come up with any money himself?"

"Nope."

"Obviously, you worked this little deal with him more than once?"

"It got to be habit-forming."

I closed my eyes long enough to do a quick computation. Feldman had to clear six thousand dollars on the three hundred outfit deal alone. In 1962, six thousand dollars was considerably more than a year's salary for an average working stiff. I could believe it got to habit-forming.

"Anything unusual about the last deal? Anything that went wrong, for example?"

"Nothing went wrong that I know of. The money came through like clockwork. The only twist was, Jerry insisted that for this deal there was an offbeat initiation fee."

"Initiation fee?"

"Yeah. Everyone involved had to make a particular bet with some bookies Jerry named."

So that was how I learned about the improvident wager that Liebniewicz was telling T. Graham about at just about the same time. I chalked it up to Celtic eccentricity. I do international commercial transactions. My betting experience stops at five dollars a year on the Harvard-Yale game.

"Any more questions?" Feldman asked.

"Just the one I came in with. Why'd you get in bed with a cheap lowballer like Corbett?"

Feldman hoisted his feet to his desk, leaned back in his chair, and smiled mordantly.

"Why did Johnny Maddox go to the river?"

I nodded and stood up. I leaned far enough across his desk to shake hands without making Feldman abandon his comfortable position. I found my own way out.

"Excuse my ignorance, Theodore," Thomas said about five minutes later, when I reached him and Sandy by phone at their apartment and related my parting exchange with Feldman. "But why did Johnny Maddox go to the river?"

"Because the river's wet," I told him. "And Beale Street'd done gone dry."

"I'm proud of you for just throwing that line away like that, Theodore. Several of my classmates would've milked an entire existentialist novel out of it."

"I'm just not the existential type, Thomas," I said. "But we need to talk about this in more detail, and the sooner the better."

"Well, at the moment I'm being pulled out the door to an Irish wake. Listen, why don't you just come over to the apartment and wait for us? I'll tell the doorman to let you in, you can put Charlie Parker or Dave Brubeck on the record player in lieu of Johnny Maddox, and as soon as Sandy and I get back we can go over everything, starting with why you poked your nose into this affair without bothering to tell us."

"Fine. If my memory of Irish wakes serves me correctly, I'll see you around two this afternoon."

All I can say is that it seemed like a good idea at the time.

145

Chapter Twenty

"It still looks like he's going to be a while," the gray-haired woman at the Underwood typewriter said to T. Graham. She tried to sound apologetic and didn't quite make it.

"That's all right," T. Graham said serenely. "I don't mind waiting."

He was standing at the window, glancing periodically from it to the receptionist/secretary's desk. Two white, rotary-dial telephones rested next to each other on the front part of her desk. Each had one red button and five clear buttons across the bottom.

The first clear button on the phone to the left glowed a steady amber. The second and third clear buttons on that phone winked amber to clear. At intervals ranging from thirty seconds to seven minutes, whichever button was glowing would go back to clear, one of the winking buttons would change to a steady glow, and the button that had just gone clear would then start blinking urgently as the phone jangled with another incoming call. The gray-haired woman would pick the receiver up, whisper, "Hold please," mechanically into the mouthpiece, and push the red button. The clear button would then change from an urgent blink to a steady wink, waiting for the cycle to be repeated.

None of which meant anything except that Louis Kovacs got lots of calls on Saturday mornings.

What intrigued T. Graham was what happened on the phone to the right. That phone had only rung once during the twenty minutes T. Graham had been in the office. But throughout that time, whether the phone was in use or not, the fifth clear button had been amber.

"Have you been working very long for Mr. Kovacs?"

"Long enough."

"He used to be a fairly busy lawyer. Mostly on the civil side. I remember running into him quite a bit in various courthouse corridors during the late thirties."

"He's still a very good lawyer," the woman said. Her tone this time dared T. Graham to contradict her.

"I'm certain he is," T. Graham assured her. "Not so much trial work any more though, I gather."

"It was the war," the woman said.

"Oh?"

"A trick knee that he picked up playing football kept Mr. Kovacs out of the service during the war."

"Trick knee, yes. Terrible things, trick knees."

"It seemed like after the war you couldn't get anywhere anymore as a trial lawyer unless you were a veteran. At least over here in Brooklyn. People didn't wanna hear about trick knees. They wanted to see that campaign ribbon."

T. Graham nodded sympathetically and looked out the window again. Half an hour later he didn't seem to have moved. It was at that point that Kovacs finally emerged impatiently from an office down a short corridor beside the desk.

"Agnes, hold my calls," he yelled, waving at her and striding at top speed toward T. Graham at the same time.

"Yes, Mr. Kovacs," the woman said.

"Ah," T. Graham said, "a pleasure, Mr. Ko—"

"Yeah, right, me too," Kovacs said in a high-speed staccato rattle. "Look, uh, Mr. Surrey, sorry to keep ya waitin'—"

"Curry."

"—but you know how it is. I got about ninety seconds that I'm stealin' from everything else, but that's all."

"That should be more than enough. Perhaps we could step—"

"No, no, I'm really runnin'. Just tell me what's on your mind 'cause I can't spare a lotta time for chat."

"Very well. How much money did you lend Jerry Fielder?"

"Never lent Jer a dime. I look like a bank to you?"

"That's curious, because I understand his companion Mr. Madden—"

"Look, I'm sorry, that was a smart-ass crack. Jerry Fielder tried to put the touch on me. Okay? More than once. Okay? An' maybe now an' then I'd shake loose with a five-spot or a sawbuck. But that's not whatcha call a loan, okay? 'Cause we shouldn't speak ill of the dead, God rest poor Jerry's soul, but those were gifts. I knew it an' he knew it."

"Mr. Madden seems to think he overheard Fielder asking you for money and saying something about the fix being in. Very shortly before Fielder passed away."

"Look, Mr. Surrey—"

"Curry."

"—I like R.J. He's a good kid. But he's a big, dumb Irish jock. They don't wear helmets in basketball, an' I think ol' R.J. took a few too many forearms to the noggin back when he was playin'. Over an' above not bein' the smartest guy in New York to begin with, I think R.J.'s maybe a coupla bricks shy of a full hod."

"So you'd say he's just remembering something that didn't happen?" T. Graham asked placidly.

"I dunno. How do I know what the kid thinks he heard?

148

Jer came by, tried to put the touch on me, I said no, okay? Maybe Jer said he'd fix things up between us if I came through or somethin', how do I know?"

"Was that why Fielder invited you to the game at the Polo Grounds? Because you'd turned him down?"

"You didn't know Jer, didya?"

"I can't say I—"

"If Jer could do a favor, he did a favor, long as it didn't cost him anything. He owed me, he'd had me on the list for that game for a long time, I went, end of story. Period. The end."

"What was in the envelope he gave you?"

"A Columbus Day card. Jer liked to get stuff out early."

"How very droll."

"Really, I look like the kinda guy's gonna answer a question like that?"

"Perhaps if the police ask it."

"Don't hold your breath. They're not interested in me as Jerry's killer. The times don't work."

"I wouldn't expect the police to find the sign-out sheet that conclusive," T. Graham said.

"The sign-out sheet's the least of it. I left around mid-game. On the way outta the park, I got to thinking about a proposition Jer'd made to me."

"In the envelope, perhaps?"

"I told ya, I'm not gonna get into that. Anyway, I call him from the first pay phone I can find, they page him, he calls back the pay phone number, we talk for a good five minutes. The police musta talked with the stadium about the times of the calls, and it musta checked out 'cause I haven't heard back from them."

"In other words," T. Graham said, "your times are corroborated, as we lawyers sometimes say."

"You could say that," Kovacs agreed.

"Thank you very much," T. Graham said. "You've been most helpful." He turned toward the door, then looked back over his shoulder. "And by all means watch out for that trick knee."

* * *

Ten minutes later, while he was riding back toward Manhattan, T. Graham reached George Monaghan on the phone. Monaghan was a chief assistant D.A. in the Kings County district attorney's office.

"Whatta ya need, counsel, an adjournment?" Monaghan asked. "Your witness Mr. Green can't make it? Which case we talking about by the way?" (The most popular ground for postponements of criminal trials invoked by New York defense counsel in that era was the unavailability of their witness, Mr. Green—meaning that they hadn't been paid yet.)

"I'm not representing anyone in controversy with your office at the moment," T. Graham said. "And I've found that if you insist on payment in advance, you never have to worry about the much cited witness Mr. Green."

"More power to ya if you're that good. What can I do for you?"

"I have a favor to ask."

"That's how I got where I am, all right, doing favors for defense lawyers. What is it?"

"I'd like to know the substance of the conversation that took place within the last month between a recently deceased individual named Jerry Fielder and a Brooklyn lawyer named Louis Kovacs—"

"You what?"

"—at the latter's office."

"I can't believe you're—"

"Understand, I don't care where you get it. I don't want to know. I don't wish to speculate about the source of the information. You don't have to reveal it."

"I don't have to do anything."

"I only want to know the substance of what was said. No follow-up, off the record, no motions, no subpoenas, no demands for production."

"How can you commit to that?"

"I already told you I'm not representing anyone charged by your office."

"Then how can you threaten motions and subpoenas?"

"I could arrange to be representing someone, I suppose," T. Graham said.

"You're suggesting my office's doing some kind of delicate information-gathering at this Kovacs character's place. If there's nothing to that you're wasting my time. And if there's something to it then you're goddamn close to blackmail."

"Close only counts in horseshoes and hand grenades, I understand."

"I'll have to check on it."

"By all means do so. I'm quite confident you'll learn I'm right. Is this evening too early?"

"Late tonight."

"Thank you, Mr. Monaghan. I'll remember."

T. Graham hung up the car phone and smiled rather coldly.

Chapter
Twenty-one

I got to Thomas and Sandy's apartment sometime between 11:15 and 11:30. The moment the doorman let
me in and left me alone I started feeling vaguely uncomfortable.

This wasn't a sixth-sense premonition like the ones the gen-
etically-selected-for-combat heroes in action-adventure stories always get. It was a reaction to being alone in someone
else's home. I was afraid that if I touched anything it'd break.

Perching myself on the living room couch, I extracted a
legal pad from my briefcase and started to sketch out some
notes about my conversation with Feldman. Ten minutes or
so of that and I started to relax a little. I was an officious
interloper in this case and Thomas was going to let me know
it, but the fact was that the Feldman interview was something he couldn't have done. Feldman wasn't a job for an
advocate with an instinct for the jugular but for a counsellor

with an intuitive feel for how unconventional commercial transactions get put together.

After a while I started whistling. I strolled almost jauntily over to the record player, remembering Thomas's comment about Brubeck. The album was propped against the turntable waiting for me. I put it on without a hitch and walked into the kitchen for a beer. I was feeling right at home.

This, in my limited experience, is almost always a bad sign.

Returning to the living room, I sat in an armchair convenient to a side table that would accommodate the beer. I started to review the notes I'd made.

That was when I felt the draft.

It came from the dining room, just sharp enough to be uncomfortable on my neck. It seemed more than a little odd. The dining room windows looked out on a fire escape.

Twisting around to look into the dining room, I saw it almost immediately. The bottom left pane in the upper half of the center window was broken out. A couple of glass shards had flown as far as the dining room table, where they glittered in the late morning light.

What I had to do was walk over to the phone, call the doorman, and tell him something had happened.

Right.

For some reason, I couldn't just react. I had to think about it, visualize what I was going to do, before I could make myself move.

Well, you can't be good at everything.

I got up and moved toward the phone. I was afraid, but I wasn't afraid of physical danger. I was afraid I was going to mess up.

I felt a sudden, increased sense of urgency—something inside me screaming, "Hurry up!"—but I didn't know why. My concentration on the phone was so total that I never saw him or heard him. I was actually reaching for the receiver when I felt a split second of searing pain at the back of my skull, saw a couple of electric-white flashes behind my eyes, and then collapsed into inky blackness.

Chapter Twenty-two

"Capitalism," the man resting his haunches comfortably on the edge of the sink said, "is a system of economic organization based on exploitation of workers by rich people."

"I believe he means us," Thomas said to Birnham.

"Ah, Danny," a man leaning against the refrigerator sighed, "you always have been a red."

"I'd rather be called a red by a rat than the other way around," Danny replied amiably, "but I'm not either one. Because socialism is an economic system based on exploitation of workers by intellectuals—and between the two I'd pick rich people. When they go too far, you just put a little muscle on them and then you sit down and cut a deal. When intellectuals go too far, the only thing you can do is shoot them."

"I like that," Birnham said. "You sound like a fella I could do business with."

"And you sound like someone who's voting for Rock-efeller."

"You bet I am," Birnham affirmed. "Rockefeller's exactly what a Republican should be—an apostle of moderation."

"A New York Republican boasting of his moderation," Danny said, "is like a eunuch boasting of his chastity. He confuses virtue with necessity."

Thomas swirled the Irish whiskey Mary Margaret had served him in a tall kitchen glass. There were five men altogether in the kitchen, all wearing dark suits, white shirts, and dark ties. Birnham was the only one Thomas knew.

"Jerry had a lot of friends," Thomas said to Birnham, as the other three men started an impassioned discussion of the teamsters strike just under way.

"Guy gets around, does what he says he's gonna do, he can pick up plenty of friends," Birnham said.

"A lot of friends and a lot of associates."

"I guess so."

"I had a feeling that the party at the game Wednesday night was more associates than friends," Thomas said.

"I suppose you could be both," Birnham commented.

"I suppose you could at that. The dividing line might be between those who left the game as soon as they'd gotten what they came for and those who stayed on."

"If that's the test, I'm in the friend category. Natalie and I stayed until the outcome was no longer in doubt, as the sportswriters say."

"You and Liebniewicz."

"I think they left maybe a little before or a little after we did, but to tell you the truth I didn't really notice. A party like that, you lose track of people. You look around and all of a sudden someone's not there."

"Like R.J.?"

"R.J. Kovacs. Corbett. Mary Margaret."

"Did you talk to Jerry before you left?" Thomas asked.

Birnham shook his head.

"Knocked on the door, said something like, 'We're gonna

call it a night, Jerry, thanks for everything,' and took off. Jerry had the door closed for a reason. I figured, man wants to be alone, he wants to be alone."

"Speaking of R.J.," Thomas said then, "you haven't seen him here, have you?"

"Can't say I have."

"Neither have I. I wonder why he didn't show."

"Couldn't tell you. You'll have to excuse me, I think I'll mingle a little bit."

Thomas nodded and took a sip of Irish whiskey. For five minutes after Birnham's brush-off he stood rather still. The clink of ice cubes in glasses and the rattle of conversation seemed to fade as he thought things over. Then he decided to do some mingling himself.

"A little overwhelming, isn't it?" Birnham said to Corbett as they gazed at the swarm of people packed into the Fielders' living room, eating and drinking to mark Jerry Fielder's death.

"Catholicism isn't generally speaking an ascetic religion," Corbett remarked, nodding. He was using his Back Bay voice this morning. "And the Irish are if anything less ascetic than most adherents to that cult. Those of us with more of an affinity for British culture find it simultaneously puzzling and fascinating."

It was Corbett's misfortune that he completed this pontification within earshot of Mary Margaret Fielder, who had just led Sandy and Thomas up to the other two.

"British culture," she said, with steel-edged, elementary school teacher archness. "If it weren't for Julius Caesar and St. Brendan, they'd still be painting themselves blue and praying to trees. I believe you gentlemen and Mr. and Mrs. Curry know each other."

"Please call me next Lent and remind me that Catholicism is not an ascetic religion," Sandy told Corbett. "I will be in the mood for encouragement."

"I can see why she appealed to Jerry," Birnham said, nodding toward Mary Margaret's retreating figure.

"Jerry told me once he felt he had something to prove because he turned eighteen just a shade too late to fight in World War Two," Thomas said. "I think Mary Margaret understood that."

"I can imagine exactly how he felt," Birnham said. "I started college under the G.I. Bill in September of 'forty-six. The freshmen vets were the most confident SOBs that campus had ever seen. We whipped the depression and we won the war. That was our attitude. Look out, world, here we come."

Corbett's expression changed from a pout to a scowl. As we found out later, he had sat out World War Two with the same trick knee Kovacs had.

"I remember that first month, there were three of us walking out of the student union together," Birnham went on. "And this senior—one of those guys who was gonna finish his degree before he went in and still had his deferment on V-J Day—he charges up and says, 'Frosh! Where-are-your-beanies?' See, freshmen were supposed to wear these little beanies their first semester there, as sort of an initiation thing. So this pimply-faced twenty-one-year-old asks us why we don't have our beanies on."

"Maladroit," Sandy said.

"I thought we were going to wet our pants laughing," Birnham continued. His eyes were shining, his face split into a broad grin as he recaptured the memory. "And finally I said something like, 'Listen, pal, this "frosh" over here is Ben, who hit beaches at Anzio and Normandy, and this other "frosh" is Chuck, who flew twenty-three missions behind the belly gun of a B-seventeen, and I'm Andy and I've been dodging mortar shells on coral reefs for over three years— and you can just take that beanie stuff and shove it right up where the sun don't shine.' "

"Ah, college days," Thomas smiled.

"I'll tell you, though, after it was all over, after I'd been out a few years, I looked back on it and I realized I'd missed out on a lot of what college was supposed to be. All of us who came out of the war had."

"I know."

"I remember, I saw the cartoon Bill Mauldin drew to close out the Willie and Joe series he'd done during the war. This one showed Willie on campus in 1946, wearing his letter sweater, smoking a pipe, sitting in the window seat of a bay window that looked out on the yard in autumn, with copies of *Moby Dick* and Shakespeare's plays lying around him."

"We can take it that it wasn't exactly like that?" Corbett asked knowingly.

"Not for us," Birnham said, shaking his head. "No pep rallies and no bonfires for the class of World War Two. No gentleman's C, no football weekends, no panty raids, no beer parties at the boat house. We studied our brains out, we took classes over the summer, took classes over term break, went like crazy to try to make up for the years we'd lost."

"And then when you got out in the real world," Corbett asked complacently, "how much help did Plato's *Republic* and Aristotle's *Prior Analytics* turn out to be?"

"Not much," Birnham grinned. "But *The Prince* came in handy."

"Jerry Fielder would've agreed with that," Thomas said. "His last operation was worthy of something out of Renaissance Florence."

"Kind of crack is that?" Birnham demanded jovially. "Guy's wake, for crying out loud."

"I don't think Jerry'd be offended," Thomas said. "I think he'd be flattered by the idea that compulsory bets as an entry fee was Machiavellian."

The jovial smile faded from Birnham's face as he glanced sharply at Thomas. If this was supposed to be a subtly nuanced signal, Corbett didn't pick it up.

"The bet was a considerable nuisance," Corbett confirmed. "I had—"

"You just didn't know Jerry as well as you thought you

did," Birnham quickly assured Thomas. A forced conviviality colored his voice. "Jerry always thought that a straight line is the most boring distance between two points. He'd never do something up front if he could find an angle to work somewhere."

"A rather elaborate angle in this case," Thomas said.

"You can say that ag—" Corbett began.

"Something funny just struck me," Birnham interrupted brusquely, again. His eyes held Thomas's in a chilly gaze. "What'd you have to do with Jerry's last operation?"

"You mean you've forgotten the stereos?"

"You asking or telling?"

"He is asking, to be truthful," Sandy interjected. "It is a curious thing to say, but ever since we heard about Jerry's death Thomas and I have been wondering exactly what role we did have in what Jerry was doing."

"Maybe you didn't have one," Birnham said.

"Then why were we at the game?" Thomas asked.

"You don't know?" Birnham demanded. "And you expect me to be able to tell you?"

"I can tell you," Corbett said triumphantly.

"Pipe—" Birnham said.

"Stop interrupting me. It's getting on my nerves." Corbett turned his body away from Birnham and toward Thomas and Sandy. "Your role was to remind Birnham and Liebniewicz of why they were going to do what Jerry wanted them to do without making any waves and without asking for more than the going rate."

"How was Thomas to accomplish that?" Sandy asked, her voice musical with feigned bewilderment.

"By being T. Graham Curry's son. By reminding anyone who knew Jerry's history that people go to prison every now and then for playing games with labor unions."

"Just a minute," Birnham insisted.

"I'm still not finished," Corbett snapped. He looked directly at Sandy, who was favoring him with the considerable powers of her undivided attention. "You see, Mr. Birnham's

159

company never has a strike. Mr. Birnham's company never has any labor problems. And every month Mr. Birnham gets a check to Harry Liebniewicz."

"Watch what you're saying, you overrated toy-seller," Birnham snapped.

"It's called a sweetheart deal," Corbett concluded serenely. "And it's a felony."

"I'm one of those enlightened capitalists Danny was talking about in the kitchen," Birnham said evenly, glancing at Thomas as he made the allusion to Danny. "I've got a union shop and I pay union scale. Same as every other truck company in New York."

"And you never have a grievance go past the shop steward level. You never have a problem getting overtime out of your drivers. You never have a work rule complaint. I know that's no coincidence, and so did Jerry Fielder."

"Liebniewicz was the organizer who got elected business manager while Jerry was doing time?" Thomas asked.

"That's right."

"There's something you should understand, Mr. Corbett," Birnham said quietly. He didn't put his elbow in Corbett's midriff. He didn't jam the knot of Corbett's tie against his throat. His tone was if anything less insistent than before. But there was something much more menacing in his unhurried voice and slightly hissing pronunciation of "misster" than a physical threat would have been. "Robert F. Kennedy sent me a letter last year thanking me for my contribution to his brother's campaign. I have a very good accountant, and he can give you an excellent reason for every penny that my company's paid to anybody over the past seven years. I have a very good lawyer, and he can beat any labor racketeering rap that any government lawyer dumb enough to bring one could think of."

"Don't put words in my mouth," Corbett said, suddenly defensive.

"I'm the one who's not finished now, Mr. Corbett. Now you listen to me. You see, Harry Liebniewicz doesn't worry

160

about audits and subpoenas and government lawyers. He worries about teamsters with tire irons. If someone accuses him of making sweetheart contracts, he's not going to prison for two years. He's going in the East River."

"I'm not accusing anyone of anything."

"I'm glad to hear that. Because if Harry Liebniewicz got the idea that you were making noises about something like that, do you know what'd happen?"

"I—"

"I'll tell you. You'd leave for work one morning and you just wouldn't get there. They'd never even find your car. They certainly wouldn't find you. And if they did they'd have to identify you from your dental work."

"Don't mind us," Thomas said into the rather leaden silence that followed. "We were just leaving."

Chapter
Twenty-three

A 1962 TV commercial for some brand of aspirin featured a cutaway cartoon of a human head in profile. Inside the head, animated images depicted three kinds of headache pain: a hammer banging on an anvil for steady, throbbing ache; a lightning bolt for sudden, shooting pain; and rope tightening into a knot for tension.

That was exactly the way I felt when I woke up enough to feel anything.

All three of them.

At once.

Figuring that it couldn't get any worse than it was, I lifted my head tentatively from the floor.

It got a lot worse.

I decided to put my head back down and think things over for a while. That's the last thing I remember until Thomas's voice.

"Steady, soldier," he was saying.

I felt my head and shoulders lift a bit without any effort on my part.

"All right?" Thomas's voice said.

"Yes," Sandy's voice said.

I felt my torso going back down. I braced myself for the jolt that would come when my head touched the carpet again, but instead of the carpet my skull nestled into a thick, soft pillow. I remember thinking what a delightful surprise it was.

I decided to open my eyes. Big mistake. Nothing but blurs, blue white flashes, and lots more pain. I closed them again. I heard Thomas's and Sandy's voices fading in and out, and I thought that their conversation didn't make much sense.

"Do not try to move . . . Hello? Doctor Gottlieb? . . . I will be back immediately. . . . Well, is this his service? Curry. Thomas Andrew Curry. . . . Where is the bowl? . . . Yes, it is an emergency. . . . Please get one of the glasses . . . Please ask him to hurry."

The conversation faded into an indistinct buzz—rather pleasant, like bees droning on a summer Sunday afternoon. I don't remember how long that lasted.

After a while, I became aware again of parts of my body other than my head. It felt as if someone had loosened my tie and undone the top button on my shirt. Despite that, my throat felt strangely constricted. All of a sudden I knew what that meant.

"Thomas," I murmured, "I'm about to lose my breakfast."

"There's a bowl right here. Prop yourself up on your right elbow and try not to move any more than you have to."

I rolled obediently onto my right side, took one deep breath, and vomited in the general direction of a pale green ceramic mixing bowl that Thomas held in place for me. When the smell of the vomit hit me, I heaved again and threw up some more. I tasted stomach acid at the back of my throat.

"I think I've gotten up everything that's coming," I said, as if this were an accomplishment in which I could take particular pride. "Sorry about the spots on the carpet."

"Don't worry about them. The rug's Persian. No one'll notice. Drink this."

I sipped 7 Up from a glass that Thomas held to my lips with his right hand while he sponged awkwardly around my mouth with a damp facecloth in his left.

"That's better," I said after I'd rinsed a thimbleful of the drink around the inside of my mouth.

"Here," Sandy said to Thomas.

She took the glass of soda from Thomas and handed him a tumbler of coppery-colored fluid.

"Now try a little of this," Thomas instructed me.

I took a modest swallow. Napoleon brandy. Several circuits in my brain began to hum efficiently again. A very pleasant glow radiated from my stomach through my upper body to my fingertips.

"Thomas, giving Courvoisier to someone in my condition is like using a Gutenberg Bible at a Las Vegas wedding."

"Damn. I *told* Sandy bar scotch'd be good enough for you. We must be out."

An impatient rapping sounded at the door a few feet away. Sandy opened it to admit a blond, blue-eyed, absurdly fresh-faced man who looked to be in his early forties. He was wearing white shorts and a cable-knit sweater. He carried a black doctor's bag.

"Good," he said, looking down at me, "you haven't killed him yet."

He knelt over me and flashed a penlight in each of my eyes.

"Tennis shorts?" Thomas said. "I thought you were one of those doctors who when he's not treating me is home studying medicine."

"Doctors like that don't make house calls," the newcomer muttered absently. He was giving all of his attention to the crown of my skull. "Say something," he directed me.

"What would you like to hear?"

"Something suggestive of lucidity."

"My name is Theodore Furst, I'm a forty-five-year-old com-

164

mercial lawyer, I'm in the apartment of my friends and colleagues Thomas and Sandy Curry, and sometime in the recent past someone hit me very hard on the head."

"Good. How many penlights am I holding in front of you?"

"One."

"Sharp or fuzzy?"

"As sharp as anything is without my glasses."

"Do you think you can sit up?"

I winced as I pulled myself to a sitting position. It hurt, but my head didn't start spinning.

"Good," the physician in tennis shorts said again. He circled behind me. I winced again as his fingers probed tender flesh.

"You lucky cuss," he said then in a mildly surprised voice. "You're not going to need any stitches. This'll sting a little."

He rubbed an astringent liquid over the tender place on my skull. I felt as if the skin just above my ears had suddenly been pulled up to the top of my scalp.

"It's acceptable to say something profane at this point," he said. He pressed into place a square, gauze-and-adhesive-tape bandage that he had just deftly made.

"If I think of anything profane enough I'll say it."

"You really should stay in the hospital overnight for observation."

"Nonsense."

"I know. I only recommended it because my malpractice insurer makes me."

He scribbled something on a prescription pad, tore the top sheet off, and handed it to me with two aspirin-sized white pills.

"Take one now and one before you go to bed, as long as you go to bed more than four hours from now."

"What are they?"

"I don't know. They're samples that the Pfizer rep gave me the last time he was by. If you die I'll know not to prescribe them for any of my regular patients."

I gulped one of the pills and washed it down with Courvoisier. I was starting to feel almost chipper.

"Don't forget to get the prescription filled tomorrow."

"I'll remember. Thank you."

"Don't thank me till you see my bill." He turned toward
Thomas. "It was forty-love when I left. Do you suppose they
waited for me?"

He shook hands, received thanks from Thomas, declined
Sandy's invitation to stay for a drink or a bite to eat, and left.

Thomas saw me start to stand up and hurried over to help
me.

"I'm not an invalid,"I protested.

"That remains to be seen."

He walked me over to the couch.

"I should call Marge."

"Sandy already talked to her."

"Good," I said decisively. "Then let me give you a quick
rundown of what I picked up this morning, and I'll head back
home."

"Why don't you give me the rundown while I fix you
something hot to eat? Alfred is already heading out to pick
Marge up and bring her in."

"Bring Marge in?"

"Well, yes, actually. She wants to see you as soon as possible and unless we forget about calling the police you're
going to be here a while yet."

"The police, of course," I sighed. "I hadn't even thought
about that."

"You've had other things on your mind. I do expect they'll
want to talk to you."

"Probably so."

"After they're through, perhaps you and Marge can have
dinner with Sandy and me and then you two can take your
car home. Or if you feel up to a night on the town, Dakota
Stratton's at the Plaza and *The Notorious Landlady* is still playing."

"Sounds exciting. I should get hit on the head more often."

"What would you like to eat right now?"

"Anything you'd care to fix as long as there's lots of it. When you mentioned food I suddenly realized I was ravenous."

"Basted eggs, toast and bacon?"

"Perfect." In 1962 only a handful of drones in the AMA worried about cholesterol.

"I guess I have a glass head," I said twenty minutes later as I cleaned up my second plateful of rich food. "Peter Gunn gets knocked out, he gets up, rubs his head, and starts chasing the bad guys again. Someone conks me and I'm a candidate for the emergency room."

"He probably uses a double for the knockout scenes," Thomas said.

In between mouthfuls of the abundant meal Thomas had provided, I'd told Thomas about Mystkowiak and Feldman and what little I had to report about the attack on me. While Thomas and I were engaged in this way, Sandy had been traipsing systematically around the apartment with a pad of quadrille-lined lab-report paper, a red pen, and a blue pen. I surmised that she was trying to figure out what whoever had attacked me had taken away with him. Being Sandy, she was going about this with the methodical thoroughness of an insurance adjuster who'd been trained by a Jesuit chess-player.

"Now, Theodore," Thomas said, and paused.

I braced myself. It was about time for him to demand—quite properly—by what right I had barged into his case without so much as telling him first.

"Uh, yes, Thomas, you see—"

"I couldn't have levered that story out of Feldman," he said. "Neither could Sandy. Neither could Dad, for that matter. I'm glad you had enough sense to jump in and get it, even though I didn't have enough sense to ask you to."

For just a moment I was speechless. I covered it up by pretending I had a piece of toast caught in my throat.

"Oh, well, Thomas," I said then with dismissive magnanimity, "all in a day's work and that kind of thing."

Sandy bustled into the kitchen where Thomas and I were talking.

"We are dealing with a very curious type of burglar," she said.

"Which of our valuables did he take?" Thomas asked.

"None of them. The sterling, the pearls you gave me, your cuff links and your gold money clip, your spare Piaget wristwatch, your revolver, the saber my father left me, and my two Italian fencing foils, our cameras—none of that is missing."

"Congratulations, Theodore," Thomas said. "You scared him away before he could get whatever he came for."

"Unfortunately not," Sandy said.

"What do you mean? I thought you said that nothing valuable was missing?"

"Nothing valuable is. What is missing is something derisory—something almost worthless."

"What?"

"The baseball scorebook that Jerry gave me the night you and I met him."

Chapter Twenty-four

"Can I get a stool, ma'am?" the first short, squat detective asked.

"Of course."

Sandy quickly fetched a two-step wooden stepladder from the kitchen and handed it through the middle dining room window to the detective on the fire escape outside it. His partner, who was also short and squat but who was standing inside the dining room, thanked her. It was close to six o'clock and the last rays of full sunlight were on the verge of fading.

"You didn't get any kind of look at him at all?" Bernstein was asking me about the same time in the living room.

I shook my head.

"He came up behind me and hit me before I could turn around."

"Probably a good thing," Bernstein nodded musingly. "Do

you remember a smell—cologne, after-shave, anything like that?"

"Sorry."

He nodded again, sympathetically this time, and started looking over his notes. I had the feeling that the note review was just an exercise, a way to let a few seconds pass before he asked the next question.

"Bingo," I heard the detective on the fire escape say.

"What is it?" his partner asked.

"Speck of electrician's tape. Some of it musta tore off when he hit the little pane here."

"Think he taped it over before he broke it?"

"Yeah. You can see here where tape that didn' tear off took some of the paint from the frame."

"Wonder where he stashed it."

"Prob'ly just threw it out the window. All the tape an' what was left of the pane."

"Pro, huh?"

"Not even a semipro. More like an apprentice. The tape shouldn' go onna the frame at all, an' he musta left some blisters in the middle. That's why a coupla chunks of glass flew inside the room."

Looking up irritably from his pad, Bernstein glanced into the dining room where the other two detectives were working and where Sandy was polishing a spoon and taking her time about it.

"You guys wanna save that crimestoppers' textbook stuff for your report?" Bernstein called.

"Sure, lieutenant."

Sandy instantly stopped polishing the spoon.

Bernstein turned toward Thomas.

"This list of valuables that Mrs. Curry has is pretty impressive," he said.

"It was one of the first things she did after she moved in," Thomas nodded. "She was in an organizing mood and she didn't quite have time to recatalog the Library of Congress so she did that instead."

"Not likely that she missed anything, is it?"

"I think not," Thomas said drily.

"So he was after the scorebook and only the scorebook," Bernstein said.

"What puzzles me," Thomas commented then, "is why whoever broke in here didn't go ahead and take a couple of watches and rings just to make us think it was a legitimate burglary."

"Had to be timing," Bernstein said. "The scorebook was what he wanted, so that's the first thing he went for. Then, before he could grab anything else, Mr. Furst got here and by the time the burglar had taken care of him he was too scared to do anything but run."

"Timing," Thomas said, nodding. "Right."

Sandy strolled in to join us.

"Why do you suppose he wanted the scorebook?" she asked.

"Your guess is as good as mine," Bernstein shrugged.

"I have no guesses," Sandy said. "I do have a suggestion."

"What's that?"

"If I can review Jerry's scoresheet from the game I am certain that I could duplicate whatever I had written in the stolen book before Thomas and I had to leave the game the night Jerry was killed."

"Why do you think that would be helpful?" Thomas wondered out loud. "They ought to show the same things. There isn't any discrepancy between what's in Jerry's scorebook and what actually happened in the game, is there?" he asked Bernstein.

"None that anyone's spotted so far. The totals are correct through the seven innings he completed."

"I have no idea how the comparison would help," Sandy said. "But the killer apparently thought that there was something in the scorebook that he needed to be sure Lieutenant Bernstein would not see—something so important that he was willing to take an enormous risk in order to purloin the scorebook."

"Ah," Thomas said. "Comes the dawn."

"If whatever the killer is worried about was put in the scorebook the night of the killing," Sandy continued, "then I am the one who put it there. Whether it is the same as what appears in Jerry's book or different, by duplicating what I put in the stolen book that night, I may make it possible for Lieutenant Bernstein to see whatever the killer was anxious for him not to see."

"It's a long shot," Bernstein sighed. "It's as long as they come. But I guess it's worth a try. Can you come down to the precinct tomorrow afternoon, say around one?"

"Certainly."

"Great. I really appreciate that, Mrs. Curry."

The other two detectives picked this point in the conversation to wander in from the dining room.

"We're all through in there," the one who had been out on the fire escape said.

"Okay," Bernstein said, getting up and tapping his notebook. His eyes were still on Thomas. "You and Mrs. Curry have any plans for tonight, or will you pretty much be around the apartment? In case we have to get back to you, I mean?"

"It's Saturday night," Thomas shrugged.

"Let me ask the question in a slightly different way," Bernstein said, smiling. "Can you give me your word that I can have twenty-four hours on this before you try to, ah, look anyone up?"

Huh? I thought. Obviously, I was missing something. Of course I'd recently been hit on the head.

"Sandy and I have tickets for tonight to *A Funny Thing Happened on the Way to the Forum*," Thomas said. "Maybe you can fill us in on how things are going when we come by tomorrow afternoon for Sandy to look at the scoresheet."

"Maybe I can," Bernstein answered as he grabbed his hat and led his two colleagues toward the door. He was still smiling when he said it. Barely.

"What was that all about?" I asked when Thomas got back

from showing the detectives out. "Giving him twenty-four hours and so forth?"

"Got me," Thomas said. "I guess it's the kind of thing cops've thought they have to say since Broderick Crawford got to be such a big hit on *Highway Patrol*. Anyone feel like a drink before dinner?"

"Emphatically," I said.

"Just one," Marge said. "And we can't impose on you for dinner after everything else you've done and all you've been through."

"But it is no imposition whatever," Sandy protested as Thomas started to mix a Manhattan for Marge. "We are—"

"I won't hear of it," Marge said firmly. She accepted her cocktail from Thomas and thanked him. "Your apartment has been broken into, you've spent the entire afternoon looking after my husband, and you have plans for this evening. I'm going to get Ted home and in bed."

"I am sure you know best," Sandy smiled.

I wasn't in any mood to argue, especially after Thomas handed me my martini a few seconds later. Just as Thomas's offer of food a few hours before had reminded me of my appetite, the reference to bed made me think about how dull my head felt and how delightful a pillow would be.

And so, less than half an hour later, still feeling just the right buzz from Thomas's martini, I sank into the passenger side of the front seat of my Oldsmobile while Marge began to drive us back toward Long Island. We were fifteen minutes into the drive before I jolted out of my semidoze and sat up straight.

"What is it?" Marge asked.

"I just realized what Thomas and Bernstein were talking about," I said. "Bernstein assumes that everyone in the apartment except me knows who broke in, and he was telling Thomas to lay off the guy. I used to watch *Highway Patrol* once in a while and Captain Dan Matthews never said anything like Bernstein did in his life."

"You're being oblique, Ted." Marge was the only one who ever called me Ted.

"I think it's all right," I said wearily, letting my head roll back into the seat cushion again. "Thomas expressly told Bernstein that he and Sandy were going to a play tonight. He said it with Sandy standing right there, and I don't think Sandy would let herself be party to an outright lie."

"Actually," Marge said thoughtfully, "Thomas didn't expressly say that he and Sandy were going to a play tonight. What he said was that they had tickets."

Chapter
Twenty-five

T. Graham scooted over on the semicircular banquette and pushed the papers he was trying to read into a small splash of light that a remote ceiling fixture threw onto the shiny black surface of the table. The point of El Morocco was dancing, so the lighting there wasn't quite as dim as in most New York nightspots. At the moment, however—about 9:45 Saturday night—Rhonda Cheshire and the Cheshire Kittens were still ten minutes or so from the end of their early set and most of El Morocco's light belonged to them. If it hadn't been for the ceiling fixture it would've been all T. Graham could do to make out the gray black type on the pages before him.

He was thoroughly familiar with transcripts like this one, characterized by a minimum of punctuation and doggedly formalistic spelling. He had used a thick-pointed pencil to substitute "Fielder" for "Voice 1" and "Kovacs" for "Subject," but apart from that he let it stand the way it had been typed:

FIELDER: I tell you Louis you got to lend me the dough.

KOVACS: I don't got to do nothing Jerry. Not where you're concerned.

FIELDER: Louis you're not hearing me. I'm telling you the fix is in.

KOVACS: I'm hearing you Jerry I'm just not listening to you.

FIELDER: I got it straight from a guy in the league office.

KOVACS: Sure you did Jerry.

FIELDER: Louis this is on the level.

KOVACS: What fix is that then?

FIELDER: So you're interested huh?

KOVACS: You want to stand there and ask stupid goddamn questions or you want to talk to me? I'm doing you a favor just sitting in the same room with you instead of throwing you out.

FIELDER: All right all right don't get sore Louis. Jesus. Okay. Here's the deal. The Mets are odds-on right now to set a major league record for losses in a single season.

KOVACS: So?

FIELDER: The league is very embarrassed about that.

KOVACS: What for? They're an expansion team. Everyone knew they'd stink.

FIELDER: Louis it's one thing to stink and another thing to be the worst team in eighty years of baseball. California's an expansion team. Washington's an expansion team. The Houston Colt Forty-fives're an expansion team. They're bad but they're not setting records. The Mets are in New York Louis. They're a national laughingstock. Steve Allen makes jokes about them. That new kid's taking over for Paar what's his name?

KOVACS: Carson.

FIELDER: Carson right. Johnny Carson. Johnny Carson makes jokes about them. America's laughing at New York's National League team. New York's National League team Louis.

KOVACS: So what?

FIELDER: I'm telling you the league doesn't like this. The league doesn't want that record set. Not by the Mets. The word's gone out. The race is over except for Frisco and L.A. and maybe Cincy. Anyone else plays the Mets after this weekend you're not going to recognize the names in the box score. You're not going to see Warren Spahn and Lew Burdette pitching against the Mets. You'll see some triple A kid called up for September. The Mets are getting set up for an amazing winning streak that'll keep them from setting the record and send their fans into the winter happy.

KOVACS: I don't buy it Jerry.

FIELDER: Louis all I need is ten g's for God sakes.

KOVACS: You don't look to me like you're good for ten cents,
Jerry.

FIELDER: Five g's Louis. Please.

KOVACS: I can't see it Jerry. Shove off. And take that muscle-
bound mick in the waiting room with you.

T. Graham folded the pages and tucked them into the inside pocket of his tuxedo jacket. He brushed his fingers re-
flectively over the silk facing on his lapel as he brought his
hand out. It would've been a lot simpler if Kovacs had said
something like, "I can go a thousand, Jerry."

He signaled across the room at a cigarette girl. She made
her way unhurriedly toward him, chirping, "Cigars, cigarettes," as she went.

"A pack of Old Gold Filter Kings," he said when she arrived.

"Twenty-five cents," she trilled, depositing the pack in
front of him and in almost the same motion scooping up the
quarter and nickel he laid down. "Thank you." T. Graham
has asked that note be made of the fact that he did not pat the
young woman's bottom as she strolled away, limiting himself
instead to visual appreciation.

"The Thomas Graham Curry I know can afford a bigger tip
than that," a masculine voice behind T. Graham said.
T. Graham glanced around.

"In the immortal words of John Maynard Keynes," he answered, "I will not be a party to any process that contributes
to the debasement of the currency. Hello, Mickey. Glad you
could make it."

Sapphire Mickey Teitelbaum clapped T. Graham heartily
on the back, pumped his right hand briskly, then wedged
himself into the banquette on the other side of the table. Not
quite six feet tall, he weighed perhaps 230 pounds. He had a

178

ring of silver hair that ran around the back of his head, and he had coaxed nine or ten strands of this pelt into growing long enough to let him comb them across the top of his otherwise bare scalp. His tuxedo jacket was powder blue with black trim and black velvet lapels. His silken bow tie was midnight blue. A thumbnail-sized sapphire glowed dully in the V formed by his lapels. A circlet of tiny diamonds sparkled from each of his cuff links.

"I dressed down like you told me," he said. "No sequins."

"I appreciate it," T. Graham said drily. "How's business?"

"Business is terrible. Couldn't be worse."

"You've been saying that for twenty years."

"I've been saying it for thirty-seven years. You've just been hearing it for twenty."

A ripple of applause signaled the end of Rhonda Cheshire's set. After a perfunctory bow and a wave to the band, the auburn-haired singer headed for T. Graham's table with one of the Kittens in her wake. The Kitten was in her early twenties. Rhonda wouldn't see forty again.

T. Graham and Sapphire Mickey stood up as the two women approached. Introductions completed—the Kitten's name turned out to be Sherry—the women slipped into the banquette in between T. Graham and Sapphire Mickey. T. Graham put the pack of Old Golds and a silk-finish El Morocco matchbook in an ashtray and slid it in front of Rhonda.

"Thanks, Graham, that was thoughtful. There's not enough room in one of these dresses for a nail file."

"You're welcome."

"What happened to your chorus girl?"

"Her sense of professionalism forbids her to go out on a night before she has a matinee."

"That's Graham," Rhonda said through a cloud of blue smoke to Sherry and Sapphire Mickey. "One night out with him and this kid hoofer's through for the weekend. She'll probably be on the wagon for three months."

Two waiters wheeled up a magnum of champagne

wrapped in a white towel and nestled in a silver ice bucket. They distributed glasses and began the elaborate process of opening the bottle.

"Hey, I take back that crack about the tip," Sapphire Mickey said to T. Graham as he glimpsed the label on the bottle. "You don't mind spending money at all."

"As you mature spiritually," T. Graham said complacently, "you come to realize that money is trivial. What really matters is sex and power."

"Money's trivial all right," Rhonda said. "As long as you have it."

"What do you do, Mr. Curry?" Sherry asked in an alto purr.

"I'm a lawyer and I own some real estate. I also do some investing now and then. The arts, mostly. Paintings. Broadway shows. That kind of thing."

"That sounds very exciting," Sherry said, her eyes widening and her voice suggesting genuine rapture.

"Don't get carried away," Rhonda told her. "It's a long way from a glass of good champagne to having your name above the title."

This admonition left Sherry unfazed.

"How about you, Mr. Teitlebaum?"

"Mickey."

"Mickey," she corrected herself. "What's your line?"

"Good question. A paper a couple of months ago said I was a gangster."

"Oh, that's horrid. Did you sue them?"

"Why should I? They spelled my name right."

"You two guys are a lotta fun," Sherry laughed. "Mickey, can I have a puff on your cigar?"

"Cripes," Rhonda muttered, "now she's doing Blanche DuBois."

"Sure," Sapphire Mickey said to Sherry. "You want one of your very own?"

"Maybe after the second show, tiger."

"That's what I wanted to hear," Mickey said.

180

"Second show," Rhonda said thoughtfully. "Yes, there is one tonight, isn't there? Pity."

"But it's not for—" Sherry started to protest.

"Time for us to scram and let the gents chat," Rhonda said firmly. "See you around midnight."

T. Graham and Sapphire Mickey rose so that Rhonda and Sherry could exit.

"Cute kid," Sapphire Mickey said as they sat back down. "Fresh and unspoiled."

"Perhaps," T. Graham said dubiously. "Or perhaps she was just glowing in the reflected light of your immense charm."

"Compliments too. Champagne, a girl who's a real dish and just my type, a night at one of the swankest spots in town, and compliments too. You must really wanna know something important."

"How important would you say Louis Kovacs is?"

"Louis the Brooklyn bookie? Louis who'd be a living legend if only he were really living? Not very. He had a shot once."

"What happened?"

"It's like the stock market," Sapphire Mickey said. "In the long run, the bulls make money, the bears make money, the only ones that lose money are the pigs. Louis has a nasty habit of betting for his own account and trying to shade the action. He'll never be a really successful gambler, and because of that habit of his he'll never be anything more than a small-time bookie."

"Who's his muscle?"

"Used to be Rastus Washington, deceased."

"Deceased how long?"

"Good seven years."

"Who replaced him?" T. Graham asked.

"No one. Louis found out he could be his own muscle. He's a pretty tough buzzard and he knows his way around. If you ask me, that's how Rastus got deceased. But you didn't hear that tonight."

"Hm."

"This helpful at all?"

"Somewhat. What can you tell me about Andrew Birnham?"

"Smart money. Probably wagers thirty thousand a year. Might come out seventy-five hundred ahead, never finishes more than five thousand behind. Doesn't believe in hunches. Bets on sports, mostly. He has contacts and brains and he knows how to use both."

"How about Harry Liebniewicz?"

"Never heard of him."

"He's a Teamster."

"Oh, that's different," Sapphire Mickey said. "Teamster headquarters in New York is sort of the Grand Central Station of anything bent going on in sports wagering. After all, those pension funds are awful juicy, and there's just so much Las Vegas real estate you can buy."

"They get involved in point-shaving and that kind of thing?" T. Graham demanded, incredulous.

"You'll never hear me say that. They *know* about it."

"Last question: B. Weldon Corbett."

"Walter Mitty. He wants to play at walking on the wild side. He thinks a hundred bucks is a major flutter. He *pays* people for advice on wagers. Not for inside information. Just for advice. He gets good enough advice, too, but he's so scared of plunging that his winnings end up being less than his expenses."

"Thank you very much, Mickey. I hope you'll excuse me for a few minutes."

T. Graham hurried to a pay phone next to El Morocco's coatroom. He dialed Thomas and Sandy's apartment and got no answer. He dialed the office and got no answer there. That's when he called me.

"Furst, do you have any idea where my son is?" he asked when he had gotten through the barricade Marge had tried to construct around me.

182

"I hope and pray that he's with Sandy at *A Funny Thing Happened on the Way to the Forum.*"

"You sound doubtful."

"I am."

T. Graham dialed the Alvin Theatre and bullied whoever answered into paging Thomas at the next scene change. No one answered the page.

"Damn," T. Graham muttered as he hung the phone up. "I hope he's not going to do something stupid."

Chapter
Twenty-six

It wasn't technically a sucker punch, because Thomas moved in head-on and gave R.J. a full second to see what was coming. The short, sharp jab caught R.J. on the left side of his face, knocking him against the front door of the Columbus Avenue Gym.

"The hell—?" he barked as he staggered upright. Rubbing his left cheek with one palm, he focused in angry surprise on Thomas, who stood a few feet away, dressed in blue jeans and a navy, crew-neck pullover. It was ten after ten, Saturday night.

"You know what the hell," Thomas said in a thick, muffled voice.

"You drunk or'd you have a reason for doin' that?"

"When I got home this afternoon," Thomas said, "I found a decent, harmless, middle-aged man whom I happen to like very much lying on the floor in a pool of his own blood. When I first saw him I thought he was dead."

"Sorry to hear it," R.J. said."What's it to me?"

Thomas answered by dancing forward fast with his fists raised. R.J. did the same thing. They pummeled each other's forearms for a second or two before R.J. locked his wrists, pushed Thomas away toward the sidewalk, and retreated a few feet in the opposite direction.

"You wanna tell me what in hell you're comin' after me for?" R.J. demanded.

"You're the one who hit Theodore Furst in my apartment this afternoon," Thomas said.

"The hell I am."

"The hell you're not. The guy who broke into my apartment had to be over six-three and he had long arms. A cop who was five-seven needed a stool to reach the window the burglar broke from the fire escape. Whoever did it knew enough about second-story work to be dangerous but not enough to be good. The only thing he was interested in was incriminating evidence about Jerry's murder. Go ahead, R.J.: Tell me it was Birnham or Corbett or Kovacs who broke in there."

"Wadn' me," R.J. said without an ounce of conviction in his voice. A lost, defensive expression masked his face.

"It wasn't anyone else, R.J. I think this is the part where you say, 'Bless me, Father, for I have sinned.' "

"Look," R.J. said, "you been down this road before. You think you got somethin' on me an' you wanna scare me into talkin' to you some more. I'm not buyin' it. Take a hike."

"Wrong. I didn't come here to talk. I came here to pound the hell out of you."

"You serious?" R.J. asked. There was no swagger in the question. He seemed genuinely puzzled, actually intrigued by the implausibility of Thomas's threat.

"Haven't you figured out yet how serious I am?"

"I mean, d'you got a gun or a knife or somethin'?"

"I have a decent right hook and a friend who should be in the hospital."

"What I'm tryin' to say is," R.J. persisted patiently, "how d'you expect to do this? What makes you think this is gonna happen? What're you givin' away, four inches an' thirty pounds an' ten years? Wadn' it you told me last night that if it's you against me I win?"

"I'm not giving away as much as Theodore Furst was. To hit me you're going to have to look me in the face."

R.J. sighed.

"You're not gonna be happy till we duke it out, are you?"

"That's what I've been trying to tell you. Down the alley to the service court in back. Let's go."

"How many guys you got waitin' for me back there?" R.J. demanded.

"As many as you have waiting for me. Would you rather do it right out here on the sidewalk? That's fine with me too."

"No. Round back is fine. After you."

Turning his back on R.J., Thomas stalked down the alley on the near side of the building. The alley gave onto an area twelve to fifteen feet square, dimly lit by second-floor lights from the buildings whose backs enclosed it. Striding over to the far corner, Thomas stopped in front of a couple of garbage cans and turned around.

R.J. stopped at the lip of the service court and warily examined the area. Then he moved forward one pace into a circle of pale yellow light.

Methodically, almost stiltedly, Thomas took off his watch and emptied the contents of his pockets onto the lid of the garbage can nearest him: key case, lighter, wallet, a handful of change, a penknife. He left the linings of the emptied pockets turned inside out. He held his hands up, palms out.

R.J. nodded his understanding of the playground ritual. Smiling self-consciously, he pulled his key ring and the rest of the usual male paraphernalia out of his own pockets and set them in his turn on a garbage can lid a few feet away from him. Raising his fists loosely to mid-chest level, he began to move deliberately toward Thomas.

"No Marcus of Queen-barry rules, moneybags," he said. "This is a street fight."

That was the last thing either of them said for a while. Men who are slugging it out only chatter with each other in the movies.

The typical street fight lasts less than ten seconds and involves no more than four punches. Thomas wanted to make this one last at least a minute and a half. From the first solid exchange he realized that that was going to be a major challenge.

Thomas met R.J. halfway, flitted backward to avoid R.J.'s windmill-left-roundhouse-right combination, then dove into R.J.'s ribs while R.J. was still hunting for Thomas's head. Thomas's left-right-left body punches brought R.J.'s arms down. That gave Thomas room to come up with the best uppercut he'd ever thrown, nailing R.J. with four tooth-rattling knuckles on the bottom of his jaw.

R.J. straightened up and rose on the balls of his feet. He stiff-legged back one step. Then his eyes abruptly cleared and he raised his arms in time to parry the left that Thomas followed up with a split second after the uppercut.

I just hit him with my best shot, Thomas thought, and he not only didn't go down, he barely blinked. I'm in serious trouble.

R.J. started to move forward and Thomas retreated, moving inexorably toward the corner of the service court where he had started. R.J. didn't have a boxer's moves but he was quick and athletic. He forgot about sweeping, soundstage punches like the first two he'd tried and relied on controlled jabs and flicks instead. Thomas caught most of these on his arms but the sheer power of R.J.'s reach and muscle forced two or three of them past his guard to clip his head. Oblique and half-spent though these punches were, they rocked him.

As Thomas sensed the corner behind him he knew that the only way to keep the fight going was to take a chance. He

187

took one. He lowered his guard, offering R.J. an unencumbered shot at his head.

R.J. leaped at the bait. He hurled his meaty right fist with his strength at Thomas's face. Thomas jerked his head back and to the right. R.J. hit nothing but air.

Thomas ducked, hunched, and swung for R.J.'s diaphragm. He missed it with his fist but got it with his elbow just as he felt R.J.'s left forearm slamming into the side of his head. The air left R.J.'s body all at once, producing a strangled gasp from him. His head reeling from the forearm shiver, Thomas tumbled to the ground, rolled into the open and came to his feet in time to see R.J. turn around to face him.

Thomas's breath was coming in shallow pants. Something red clouded everything he saw out of his right eye. After two deep breaths R.J. started again to move toward him, and Thomas again circled in retreat.

Suddenly R.J. skipped forward, jabbing with his left fist. Thomas raised his left arm to block the punch but his left arm was aching and tired by now and he didn't raise it fast enough. R.J.'s left slipped over the parry to slam Thomas between the eyes. Thomas's head snapped backward. He was already on his way down when R.J.'s right fist pounded into his cheekbone. When Thomas's back finally hit the pavement he was three feet farther away from R.J. than he had been when R.J. threw the second punch.

Thomas wasn't quite out. He heard R.J.'s steps scuttling across the pavement toward him. Operating on nothing but instinct and adrenaline, Thomas lurched at a garbage can that his shoulder had hit, tipped it onto its side, and rolled it at R.J.

R.J. barked his shins on the bulky obstacle. Trying to regain his footing, he slipped on the greasy trash that spilled from the can and sprawled headlong. By the time he was back on his feet, Thomas had crawled two yards away and was standing again himself.

Deliberately, R.J. turned. He was also panting now, grimacing as he tried to gulp in more air.

He took one step toward Thomas. Thomas didn't move. He took a second step and raised his fists. Thomas still didn't move. Only when he started his third stride did Thomas plunge forward, head down, arms pumping with the last ounce of endurance he had, in a final effort to make his body blows count.

He landed two before R.J. caught him on the temple with a slashing left. Thomas began to topple. R.J.'s right hit him flush on the ear. Thomas collapsed as his legs turned to jelly.

For two full seconds, R.J. stood over the bleeding, fallen man, his fists still clenched, his hard, supple body still tense, as if he expected one more assault from Thomas. With the fight finally over, he seemed unsure about what to do next.

"All right," a clear voice from the alley said. "Get out."

R.J. looked over and saw Sandy standing there, rigid as a West Point plebe taking his first brace.

"This wadn' my idea," R.J. said.

"No one said that it was. Please leave."

"You been standin' there all this time?"

Sandy offered R.J. that patented Gallic shrug that says, what can you tell someone who asks such stupid questions? R.J. looked down once more at Thomas, then turned and shuffled toward the garbage can near Sandy where the contents of his pockets lay. As he retrieved his belongings he tried and failed to meet the young woman's eyes.

"I'm sorry," he said.

"For Thomas—or for what you did to Mr. Furst?"

Shaking his head, R.J. moved back down the alley, toward Forty-second Street.

Sandy hustled over to Thomas, who pulled himself to his knees and sat back on his heels. He reached into his mouth and pulled a blood-soaked wad of cotton from between his upper gum and his cheek. Similarly sodden cotton bunches came from the other sections of his mouth while Sandy swabbed blood away from the swollen laceration over his right eye.

"Did I hold him for ninety seconds?" Thomas asked.

"You held him for over two minutes. Please hush."

Thomas shut up and submitted for another half-minute to his wife's delicate ministrations.

"There," she said at last.

Pressing fingertips to his temples, Thomas stood up.

"Are you certain you are all right?" Sandy asked anxiously.

"Are you kidding? My mother used to hit me harder than that for ordering burgundy wine with lobster."

"Please quit clowning."

"I take it you got in."

"The fight would have been over much sooner if I had not."

"Let's go."

After retrieving Thomas's watch and other effects they trekked halfway down the alley to the Columbus Avenue Gym's side entrance. Sandy pulled open the door, which she had a few minutes earlier unlocked with R.J.'s key while R.J. and Thomas were otherwise engaged.

Sandy flicked on a flashlight and handed it to Thomas. They made their way to the stairs and hurried to the basement. The door to what had been Jerry Fielder's office stood open.

"Start with the file cabinet," Thomas said as they hurried into the office.

Sandy went systematically through the four file drawers while Thomas rifled the desk.

"Any luck?" he asked after about ten minutes.

"Yes and no," she answered. "I believe I have found the file on Jerry's last business affair. But I cannot find the score-book."

"Neither can I. That doesn't prove he didn't take it."

In the moment of silence that followed, Thomas and Sandy glanced at the thin, manila file folder Sandy held. It looked at the moment like a paltry payoff for the pounding Thomas had endured to get them into the office a second time.

"Thanks to Theodore," Thomas said in a somewhat discouraged tone, "I guess we already know most of what's in there."

"*Evidemment*," Sandy said. "But if we take this with us and examine it carefully, perhaps we can figure out what Kovacs's role in the transaction was. That is one thing we certainly do not know yet."

"We won't know until we try," Thomas nodded. "Let's go."

"Very well. And there is one other thing we will take, of course."

"Of course. What's that?"

"The ribbon from the typewriter, naturally."

"Naturally. Why?"

"So that we can find out what was typed on this machine, probably for the past month if we have to. It was one of France's favorite intelligence techniques in Algeria."

"Well," Thomas sighed as he pulled the top off the old manual and began to remove the two ribbon spools from it, "you can't argue with a record like that, can you?"

September 30

KENNEDY FEDERALIZES MISSISSIPPI'S
GUARD; MOBILIZES TROOPS, ORDERS
STATE TO YIELD
New York Times, September 30, 1962, p. 1, col. 1

CASTRO ACCUSES U.S. LEGISLA-
TORS—ASSERTS CONGRESSMEN SEEK
TO PUSH NATION INTO WAR
New York Times, September 30, 1962, p. 38, col. 1

DAVE BECK, FORMER PRESIDENT OF
THE INTERNATIONAL BROTHER-
HOOD OF TEAMSTERS, TWO TRUCK-
ING COMPANY OFFICIALS AND THREE
CORPORATIONS WILL GO ON TRIAL
TOMORROW IN FEDERAL COURT ON
CHARGES OF HAVING VIOLATED THE
TAFT-HARTLEY ACT.
New York Times, September 30, 1962, p. 76, col. 3

Chapter
Twenty-seven

"J ust getting back from church, Mrs. Curry?"
Lieutenant Bernstein asked as Sandy approached her and
Thomas's apartment building. While speaking he folded up
the Sunday *New York Times* sports section that he had read
through while he waited, and opened the outside door of the
building for her.

"No, actually," she said, glancing at her watch, where she
saw that it was 10:47. "I am just returning from breakfast. I
attended mass at eight-thirty. Thomas met me at the Plaza for
breakfast afterward."

"And came home separately?" Bernstein looked puzzled.

"No. He had some work he wished to do at the office."

"I see. Do you have a few minutes?"

"Certainly. Would you like to come up?"

"Much obliged."

They rode the elevator in silence and once in the apartment

Bernstein declined Sandy's offer of coffee or tea. He leaned against the jamb of the kitchen door and watched with detached interest as Sandy laid her missal and her own copy of the *Times* on the kitchen table and began brewing tea for herself.

"I've come up with a variation on the idea you had about the scorebook," he said, once she was well into this process.

"Oh? And what is that?"

"I've checked with WNBC and they still have Wednesday night's game on tape. Before you look at Jerry's scorebook, I'd like you to listen to that tape—and while you're listening, see if you can score the game up to the time you and Mr. Curry left."

"I see," Sandy nodded. "You fear that if I look at Jerry's scorecard first, I will unconsciously 'remember' writing the same things he did and simply duplicate whatever he put down—"

"Yeah."

"—thereby defeating the purpose of the entire exercise."

"Uh, right," Bernstein said. "I hope—"

"You are entirely correct," Sandy said briskly. "I should have had the same thought myself."

"I'm having the tape delivered to the broadcast booth at the Polo Grounds. I could've had them bring it down to the precinct, but I know they've got the right equipment at the stadium and I wanted to take another look at the layout in the press box anyway. So I thought if it wouldn't be too much trouble—"

"To go to the stadium? It is no trouble at all. That will be fine."

"Great. I'll have you picked up about one."

"That is not necessary," Sandy said as she squeezed lemon juice into a cup of steaming Constant Comment. "I can find my way."

"It *is* necessary, actually," Bernstein said apologetically as he stepped aside to let her pass into the living room. "There's a Giants game there this afternoon and it'll be very crowded."

196

"A what?" Sandy asked. "But I thought the Giants were in San Francisco now."

"I'm sorry. The football Giants. They're still in New York. They'll never abandon this city. They'll be playing at the Polo Grounds forever."

"Very well," Sandy shrugged, having understood not a particle of what Bernstein had just said. "I will be waiting downstairs at one o'clock. Will that be all?"

"No, it won't, to tell the truth," Bernstein said. He took a pipe from his right-hand coat pocket.

"I thought not."

"You thought not?" Bernstein had begun patting his other pockets, and this activity now took on a certain dismayed urgency.

"Correct. You could have called with this business about the tape. If you took the trouble to come over here and wait for me, there must be something more critical. Have you lost something?"

"I must've left my tobacco pouch in the car."

"There are cigars in a humidor on the dining room buffet," Sandy said. "And some cigarettes in the box on the coffee table. The cigarettes are French and may not be to your taste."

"Thank you very much." Bernstein took one of the Caporals, then lifted the cigarette box toward Sandy.

"No, thank you," she said. "I smoke only in the evening."

"Only in the evening." Bernstein gazed thoughtfully at her for a moment. "I read where Debbie Reynolds is the same way. Bourgeois custom, I guess."

"If you like. Inasmuch as the bourgeoisie has accounted for ninety-five percent of the progress of the human race over the last two hundred years, bourgeois customs perhaps have something to commend them."

"Tell me something," Bernstein said then. "Is there any topic ordinary enough that you'd just discuss it on its own terms, instead of bringing up some profound historical or philosophical allusion?"

"I am not certain," Sandy answered, her tone studiedly

197

neutral. "I was raised in a culture that believes ideas are important for their own sake."

"Ideas like telling the truth?"

"Yes, among others."

"But that particular idea isn't one you take seriously enough to let it interfere with your husband staging a grandstand play for your benefit?"

After a leisurely sip, Sandy set down her teacup and stood up from the chair where she'd been sitting. She folded her arms across her chest. She was beginning to think that perhaps a cigarette wouldn't have been such a terrible idea after all, but she wouldn't have taken one now to save her life.

"What do you mean by that, please?" she asked, her voice clipped and icily polite.

"I mean that picking a fight with R.J. wasn't the smartest way to get back into Jerry's office, but it was a very dramatic response to R.J.'s suggestion that your husband was cheating on you."

"Your statement is inaccurate and your suggestion is implausible," Sandy said. "We could not have gotten in as we did before because we could not have been certain of procuring R.J.'s absence from the premises. *D'ailleurs*, I have complete faith in Thomas and Thomas knows it."

"Complete?"

"That is what I said."

"Mrs. Curry, I won't pretend I could read your eyes when you first saw that message accusing Mr. Curry of adultery. But you're far too intelligent not to have had at least a smidgen of doubt."

"Faith is an act of will, not an intellectual exercise," Sandy snapped. Then, after a deep breath, she continued, speaking more slowly. "Like all virtues, faith is defined in terms of the obstacles it overcomes."

"Cosmic abstraction again," Bernstein sighed. "Did you learn that during your freshman year at the Sorbonne?"

"No. I learned it last night outside the Columbus Avenue Gymnasium."

198

"You never let facts get in the way of a snappy comeback, do you?"

"I meant exactly what I said. Thomas showed courage last night when he fought R.J. Agreed?"

"Walking fearlessly into a titanic mismatch doesn't show courage, it shows stupidity."

"There was nothing fearless about it. Thomas was afraid from the moment he began his preparations. He showed courage precisely because he *was* afraid, and went ahead anyway."

"What's your point?"

"Without fear there is no courage. Without doubt there is no faith."

"Ten in metaphysics, Mrs. Curry, but zero in ethics. Mr. Curry deliberately tried to mislead me when I asked him to lay off R.J. for twenty-four hours. I know it wasn't technically a lie and I know you didn't tell it—"

"It was a lie," Sandy said, "and it was as much my lie as Thomas's. The words he spoke were true, but his intention in speaking them was to deceive you. I acquiesced in the deceit by my silence."

"At least you don't rationalize."

"Nor do I express contrition. I did it, I am glad I did it, and if I had it to do over I would do it again."

"You are an extremely dogmatic young woman."

"So I have been told."

"You know," Bernstein said then, "when I started out as a cop, about ninety percent of the people we arrested were Catholic. Italian and Irish, mostly. Of course, so were about ninety percent of the people who did the arresting. America takes both her cops and her criminals from the immigrant classes."

"Speaking of banal subjects and cosmic allusions," Sandy said, loosening up a bit.

"The thing is, I learned some things about those people. And one of the things I learned about Irish Catholics is that it's just when you think you're dealing with a dumb mick who's barely got enough brains to count his rosary beads that you're most likely to get outsmarted."

"I would not have thought of Jerry Fielder as brainless," Sandy said.

"I'm talking about R.J."

"What about him?"

"Has it occurred to you," Bernstein asked, "that everything you and Mr. Curry have found out from him are things he already knew?"

"It seems obvious," Sandy conceded, "though I cannot say we have thought of it in exactly that way."

"And have you considered that in asking him those things you've provided him with a critical piece of information that he probably wouldn't have been able to figure out for himself?"

"Namely?" Sandy prompted.

"Namely, that the things you've been asking about are the things he should factor into his thinking if he wants to puzzle out who killed Jerry—or if he wants to cover up the fact that he killed Jerry himself."

"I cannot disagree," Sandy said after a moment's reflection.

"One of my men was supposed to be keeping an eye on R.J. today. While I was waiting for you I got word that R.J. had given my guy the slip."

"I see," Sandy said evenly. "Then we should get to work as soon as possible, no? Should we leave for the stadium immediately?"

"Before we think about that—are you sure you've told me everything you know about this case?"

Sandy walked over to the desk in the far corner of the living room, unlocked the top, right-hand drawer, and took out a manila folder with a page of quadrille-lined lab report paper covered by handwriting paperclipped to it. Marching briskly back toward Bernstein, she handed it to him.

"I have now," she said.

"What's this?"

"The file on Jerry's last business affair, which we discovered in his office. On top is a memo summarizing what is in there. I was going to bring this to you when I came to look at Jerry's scorecard—though since you have already convicted me of deceit you will have to accept that assurance on faith."

"There is no faith without doubt," Bernstein said gravely. "Or at least so I've been informed."

"Fair enough," Sandy agreed, grinning.

"Let's stick with the one o'clock plan," Bernstein said then. "It's already set up that way, and I'd like to digest this before we proceed with the scorecard business."

"Suit yourself," Sandy shrugged.

"Thank you," Bernstein said. "I will."

Chapter Twenty-eight

Sunday, 1:15 P.M.

"Polo Grounds!" Thomas shouted over the phone at me, his usually cultivated voice reaching an upper register in a combination of outrage and astonishment. "What in the world are you doing at the Polo Grounds?"

"Preparing with my twelve-year-old son to watch the Detroit Lions play football with the New York Giants, as I promised him more than a month ago we would," I answered. "What are—"

"Theodore, you should be home in bed. Or at least bundled up on the couch, drinking hot buttered rum and watching football on television."

"You sound exactly like Marge. Except that she calls me Ted. She even offered, quite heroically, to take David to the game herself and pretend to enjoy the experience, even though she couldn't tell a flanker from a fullback."

"She was talking sense."

"To be perfectly honest, part of the reason I insisted on going was to escape the stifling cocoon of feminine solicitude I felt surrounding me. Somehow I feel it surrounding me again, courtesy of the American Telephone and Telegraph Company. Now: What are you doing at the office? Or, to ask the same question in a different way, how was *A Funny Thing Happened on the Way to the Forum?*"

"Very funny."

"I knew that from the reviews."

"I was referring to your question, Theodore. I'm here at the office because I want to check what we've learned from Jerry's documents against Sandy's notes about the rest of the case. Her notes happen to be here."

"What did you find out from the purloined file?"

"Nothing terribly productive. I can't see any evidence that anyone was shorted. The individual shares check out to the penny against the underlying documentation."

"What about Kovacs's role in the stereo deal?" I asked.

"He didn't have any role in that as far as I can see."

"Not even financing it?"

"Nope. The only mention of him that I can find is something I took off the typewriter ribbon: 'Dear Louie: It's been a pleasure doing business with you. Sincerely, Jerry Fielder.' "

"Dad?" David said then, tugging at my arm. "The game's about to start."

"I have to go, Thomas. I'll try to call you back at halftime."

I hung up and found my way with David to the firm's fair-to-middling season ticket football seats, three-fourths of the way up in the lower deck, around the twenty-five-yard line. I'm not really much of a professional football fan, but following the Giants back then was part of being a male New Yorker, whether you actually cared much for the game or not. Y.A. Tittle, Del Shofner, and Sam Huff for us. Yale Larry, Milt Plum, Alex Karras, and Nighttrain Lane for them. No instant replays and no Roman numerals. Just grass and mud and elemental, East Coast/Midwest football. Not a spectacle yet. Just a game. We didn't know then that Karras would be suspended six months later for betting on football games.

I had the feeling that the case was about to break. But as I watched the team captains line up for the coin-toss ceremony I didn't have any idea who was going to break it.

"Hello, everybody," T. Graham said at that moment, settling into the third of the firm's four seats. "Theodore, I think there's something we should talk about."

2:01 P.M.

". . . Braves conceding the run early in the game, the Mets have a chance to tie the score," Lindsey Nelson's voice said through the speaker. "Throneberry with a modest lead off third, standing in foul territory. Hickman leads from first after reaching on Mathews's error. Here's the one-one pitch to Elio Chacon. . . . Hard-hit ground ball to the left side, McMillan up with it in the hole, to second, one—that's all they're going to get. Bolling doesn't even try the throw to first, Chacon had it beat. Throneberry scores to knot the game at one, Hickman cut down short to second, Chacon safe at first with a run batted in on the fielder's choice force play."

Opposite Chacon's name in the second inning column on her scoresheet, Sandy drew a thin pencil line from home to first and wrote, "FC 6-4 RBI." Opposite Throneberry's name she drew a thin line from third to home. Perhaps three hundred yards from T. Graham, David, and me, without having any idea we were there, Sandy and Bernstein were huddled around a tape player in the press box booth where Jerry Fielder had been killed.

"Two out now with a runner at first for Chris Cannizzaro. The Mets could really use an extra-base hit with pitcher Roger Craig due up next."

"You can say that again," Bernstein muttered.

". . . Braves are playing Chris to pull, if he puts one in the

204

gap Elio Chacon could run all night. Strike one, slider on the outside corner." A smattering of rhythmic applause sounded in the background. "The faithful throng here at the Polo Grounds offers some encouragement to their Mets and to Cannizzaro, who has been hitting well in September. Breaking stuff high, the count is even."

"Are you having any trouble following the broadcast?" Bernstein asked.

"It was more of a challenge than I expected," Sandy admitted, "but I think I have gotten the important parts."

"If it's any consolation, there're people who've lived in New York for sixty years and don't have the faintest idea what Nelson's saying half the time."

". . . fly ball to right-center, not very deep. Maye coming in on it and makes the catch to end the inning. For the Mets, one run, no hits, one error, and one left on base. At the end of two, Braves one, Mets one."

Sandy put "8" opposite Cannizzaro's name and at the bottom of the column wrote "1/0" in the run/hit summary box. Then she reached over to the tape recorder and pushed the stop button.

"My recollection is that Thomas and I left after the top of the next inning,"she said. "I would like to check what I have so far against Jerry's scorecard and see how it matches up."

"Seems reasonable," Bernstein nodded.

He pulled a shopworn booklet from a brown envelope. It wasn't a C. S. Peterson Scoremaster Scorebook but a bare-bones scorecard like those sold at the stadium before every game. It only took a minute or so to verify that that scorecard recorded the same fates for the first seventeen batters in Wednesday night's game as Sandy had.

For another forty seconds or so, Sandy gazed intently at the two pages on which she had recorded in baseball's universal code the first two innings of the Braves/Mets game four days before.

"The matchup is perfect," she said, "but I find this profoundly unilluminating."

"So do I, I'm afraid."

"Still, there must have been *something* in my scorebook that was extremely important if someone was willing to take such an incredible risk to procure it. There must be something we are not thinking of."

"You may be right, Mrs. Curry, but—"

"Or, perhaps, something that might have been," Sandy said thoughtfully.

"Excuse me, Mrs. Curry? Could you run that one by me again?"

"Thomas and I know that we left after the top of the third inning Wednesday night," Sandy interrupted impatiently. "But the killer does not necessarily know that. The killer presumably had more important things to worry about that night than our whereabouts."

"Okay," Bernstein said in a long-drawn-out way. "I think I know where you're going on this."

"The killer did not know that my scorebook stopped halfway through the third inning. There may have been something that *could* have been in there that the killer was worried about—something about the scoring later in the game. I would like to continue your experiment with the tape recording of the game."

"Through the end of the game?"

"Yes, if necessary."

Bernstein punched the play button.

2:10 P.M.

"How did you know the phone was tapped?" I asked T. Graham after I'd run through the transcript.

"I didn't know the phone was tapped. I still don't, although I suppose we can safely assume that it is. What I knew was that the office was bugged. My guess would be a spike mike driven into the wall, transmitting to a tape re-

206

corder hidden in that second phone on the receptionist's desk—the phone whose call lights didn't operate quite the way they should have."

"How could they have something like that set up without the receptionist knowing about it?" I asked.

"I'm quite sure she does know about it. Based on what little I know of the gentleman, I'd think that the average secretary would sell Louis Kovacs out for a pack of cigarettes. Unfiltered."

"So," I said, "this suggests that Jerry Fielder didn't go to Kovacs to finance the stereo deal. He went to him to borrow money for a bet."

"Not a very shrewd bet," T. Graham said.

"That's what Kovacs thought anyway. He didn't bite. And he was right. The Mets tied the record with the loss Wednesday night and the next night the Mets lost to the Pirates and set a new major league record for losses by a team in a single season."

"And if he didn't bite," T. Graham said, "it's rather hard to come up with a motive for him."

"For him, perhaps, but maybe not for some of the others," I said.

"What do you mean?"

"All of the people in the stereo deal said that Jerry made them put up a few hundred dollars with bookies he named on a bet he specified. Maybe it was—"

"What did you just say?" T. Graham demanded.

"Birnham, Liebniewicz, Corbett, even Feldman—they all had to place bets under Jerry's control in order to take part in the stereo deal. It might've—"

"They *all* did?"

"That's right."

"Salting the mine," T. Graham murmured. "When Liebniewicz mentioned it it went right past me."

"I beg your pardon?"

"Theodore, you haven't represented enough hustlers in

your career. Let me give you a brief, guided tour of the real world."

2:25 P.M.

Fifteen minutes before, Thomas had swallowed two aspirin and a scotch neat. He wasn't sure which, but one of the two remedies had gotten rid of his headache. His brain clear, he turned a legal pad sideways on the desk before him, uncapped a black fountain pen, and began drawing a chart. When he'd finished, it looked like this:

SUSPECT	MOTIVE?	OPPORTUNITY?	CAPABILITY?
Liebniewicz	Blackmail	Yes	Yes
Birnham	Blackmail	Yes	Yes
Corbett	?	No	No
Kovacs	?	No	?
R.J.	Resentment/?	No*	Yes
Mary Marg.	Jealousy/?	No*	?

*Unless R.J./Mary Margaret is lying.

"Sandy would be proud of me," he said to himself as he looked the methodical, systematic chart over. "But it doesn't prove a damn thing."

2:40 P.M.

". . . Ashburn pounds his glove and makes the catch near the line. Any fly ball near the line is an adventure in the Polo Grounds, but Richie handles that one and that'll do it for the Braves in the top of the fifth. No runs, one hit, no errors and one runner left on base. Halfway through tonight's contest the Mets continue to hang on to a two-one lead."

Opposite Joe Adcock's name in the fifth inning column, Sandy wrote "9." In the summary box at the bottom of the column she put "0/1." She laid down her pencil, closed her eyes and rubbed them with her fingertips. If there was a pattern, it hadn't come to her yet.

3:05 P.M.

I called Thomas during halftime as I'd promised to do. He grasped the significance of what T. Graham had told me a lot faster than I had. While I was on the phone with him, he revised the Kovacs line on his chart. Under Motive he crossed out the question mark and wrote "Revenge." Under Capability he crossed out the question mark and wrote "Yes."

"Which would all be very neat," he muttered to himself after he'd hung up, "if it weren't for the 'No' under Opportunity." He drummed the pen on the legal pad. He knew he was missing something and he was irritated with himself for not being able to pick it up.

"One thing's certain," he said then in a normal tone as he stood up. "I'm not going to figure it out sitting here."

He picked up the chart and the photocopies that he'd made of the stereo file. As he walked out of Sandy's office, where he'd been working, and passed mine, it occurred to him that this collection of miscellaneous, unfastened paper was a trifle awkward to carry around. He stepped into my office and appropriated the first file he saw so that he'd have something to stuff the odd pages in while he was on his way to the Polo Grounds. The file he picked up was a thin one, labeled "Schellenwerk/Spindle Lathe Suit."

3:12 P.M.

"There," Mary Margaret said, shoving a wad of twenties and tens into R.J.'s jacket pocket. She snapped shut the briefcase she had taken the money from and tucked it back into the rear of her hall closet. "Four hundred should hold you. Get in touch with me when that runs out."

"I don' need that much."

"Don't tell me what you need."

"Okay." R.J. smiled awkwardly. "I didn' mean for it to work out this way."

"What's done is done."

"Yeah." He held out an oblong booklet. "You take this."

"What is it?"

"It's Jerry's scorebook. The one he gave the French girl."

"You haven't gotten rid of it?" Mary Margaret gaped at R.J. "You're more of a fool than I gave you credit for, Madden."

"I know. I just couldn't bring myself to dump it."

"Give it to me then."

"All right. I won' tell you where I'm goin'."

"I know where you're going. I haven't been working-class Irish for thirty-four years for nothing. You're going on a merchant steamer with a Liberian flag and an Irish captain. Be on your way."

"Okay." R.J. tried to grin and didn't bring it off. He shuffled away from the Fielder apartment and didn't look back.

Mary Margaret Fielder took the scorebook into the bathroom, laid it open on the edge of the sink, and tore out the first page. Fishing a cigarette lighter from her skirt pocket, she flicked it and set the page on fire. When it had burned to a charred scrap she dropped the remains into the toilet.

Men, she thought bitterly. Childish, sentimental fools.

She tore out the second page and ignited it. She knew that when R.J. made contact with the steamer, the captain would be looking in the face of a murderer.

3:53 P.M.

". . . Chacon quickly to his right, comes up with the ball and pegs to first. In time to nip Frank Bolling. Milwaukee is finished in the seventh. No runs on one hit, the single by Jones,

210

no errors and Jones was stranded at first base. At the end of six and a half, Milwaukee three and the Mets two."

Sandy wrote "6-3" opposing Bolling's name in the seventh inning column and put "0/1" in the summary box.

3:55 P.M.

"So you're saying Fielder hustled Kovacs," I said to T. Graham.

"That's right. He planted the idea with Kovacs that the last half of September was rigged to keep the Mets from setting a record for losses. Kovacs figured he had no reason to help Fielder get in on that action, but if it checked out he was very interested in picking up a piece of it for his own account."

"Then Fielder had some smart money bet on the Mets with several different bookies to make it look like he might be onto something."

"Exactly. Kovacs undertook his own inquiries with plugged-in bookies, found out that there was a respectable amount of unexplained action by sophisticated people in that direction, drew the conclusion that Fielder wanted him to draw, and plunged in."

"In other words," I said, "Kovacs did have a motive, at least if he figured that Fielder had sucked him in."

"If he had any doubts on that score, the message Thomas thinks Fielder gave him at the game Wednesday night should have taken care of them."

" 'It's a pleasure doing business with you,' " I nodded. "I think you're right. It only leaves three unanswered questions: Why was the sign-out sheet stolen? Why was the scorebook stolen? And how could Kovacs have managed to kill Jerry Fielder in a press box at the Polo Grounds during the eighth inning when he'd left that particular locality in the fifth or sixth?"

"I don't know the answers to any of those questions yet," T. Graham said. "But while you and Master David watch the rest of the fourth quarter, I'm going to try to get in touch with Lieutenant Bernstein."

4:15 P.M.

R.J. got off the IRT subway at Fourteenth Street and sprinted for the stairs to the BMT platform. If you just missed a train on a Sunday afternoon you might have twenty minutes to wait for the next one. Especially a Brooklyn train.

The way he felt right now, twenty minutes would seem like two hours. He felt as if people were watching him. His back tingled and he had to suppress the urge to look over his shoulder.

He had an unpleasant quarter-hour to think while he stood on the BMT platform. What he thought about was skipping the Brooklyn trip and just making for the docks. He felt himself getting physically ill. His feet twitched toward the stairs.

Then the train roared in. He stepped through the open doors, found a seat, and waited for the subway to lurch toward Brooklyn.

4:17 P.M.

". . . two shots left and only one run down at the moment, but the Mets are in a major league pickle now. Maye at second and Bell at first with *no*body out. Burdette, the Milwaukee pitcher working on a complete game, is coming up to bat now in an obvious sacrifice situation."

"Not long to go now," Bernstein said.

"For better or worse," Sandy agreed.

"Mantilla set to charge from third, Throneberry from first. Moorhead on in relief of Craig in the stretch position, checks the runners. Burdette squares around for the bunt, he's not making any bones about it, he's bunting. Here's the pitch. Bunted toward the left side. Moorhead after the ball. He's going to have a play at third! They're going to have a shot at Maye! Moorhead throws to Mantilla—oh, *not* in time. Oh, *my*.

Maye beats Moorhead's peg to third and everybody's safe. Should have had him. Now the bases are loaded and still no one out. Boy oh boy."

Mechanically, Sandy wrote opposite Burdette's name in the eighth inning column "FC 1-5 sac" and drew lines to show the runners' advance. Fielder's choice, pitcher to third/ sacrifice. She glanced distractedly at Fielder's scorecard and at first didn't even realize what she saw. She had already looked back to her own scorebook when she froze.

"Wait a minute," she said.

"What is it?" Bernstein asked.

She hit the stop button.

"Look at what Jerry's card says for that last play," Sandy said, pointing to the appropriate square.

" 'E-1,' " Bernstein read. "Error on the pitcher. Isn't that right? From the way Nelson called the play it sure sounded like an error."

"It certainly is not correct," Sandy said. "The play was not an error. There was no physical misplay. The pitcher did not pull the third base player off the base or overthrow him or fumble the ball picking it up. He simply made a poor decision in throwing to third instead of first."

"But it was because of that bad decision that he failed to get an out when he could have gotten one," Bernstein protested. "Why isn't that an error?"

"Baseball regards only physical errors as errors. Mental mistakes are not counted in that category. The proper scoring for this play is fielder's choice/sacrifice."

"But no out was made."

"An out is usually made on a fielder's choice, but it need not be. All that matters is that a play be attempted on a preceding runner instead of on the batter."

"I suppose you may be right," Bernstein said. "But I've been at least casually following the game all my life and I've never picked that up. It's a fairly subtle point, isn't it?"

"In general, perhaps. Not for Jerry, though. He knew the most technical rules even better than I do. He would never have made a mistake like that. Jerry Fielder did not fill out this scorecard."

"At least the eighth inning," Bernstein said.

"No," Sandy said, "that is precisely the point. Jerry did not fill out any part of it. The killer filled out this entire scoresheet, so that the printing throughout is internally consistent."

"We checked that," Bernstein nodded.

"As the killer assumed you would. That is why he had to steal my scorebook."

"I don't follow you."

"The killer did not care about anything I had written down. He cared about the scoresheets from earlier games that Jerry had scored. He needed to steal my scorebook so that the printing on the scorecard he planted with Jerry could not be compared with known examples of Jerry's actual scoring."

"How did the killer score the early innings? From memory?"

"No. He copied Jerry's scorecard up to the point where he'd killed Jerry. He could do that in five minutes. Then he filled in one or two more innings to cement his alibi."

"In other words," Bernstein said, "we no longer have any basis for assuming that Jerry was still alive in the eighth inning."

"Exactly."

After a knock on the door, a uniformed officer put his head inside the booth.

"What is it?" Bernstein asked.

"Excuse me, lieutenant, but some guy named Curry's tryin' to reach you so bad he's havin' kittens over it."

"You have the number he's calling from?"

"Not really."

"What's that supposed to mean?"

"Seems he's callin' from a pay phone here at the stadium."

"Have him come on up," Bernstein sighed. "The more the merrier."

The football game was over and the stadium was rapidly emptying. Thomas, T. Graham, Bernstein, and I were crowded into the press box booth that Bernstein and Sandy had been using. Sandy had wandered off. David was experiencing the delights that only a twelve-year-old can derive from a chat with a uniformed policeman with a real .38, a real set of handcuffs, and a gift for gab.

On the desk in front of the rest of us lay the planted scorecard, the scorecard Sandy had filled out while listening to the tape, and Thomas's chart. The four of us had studied them in silence for a good five minutes without achieving any more stunning breakthroughs.

"All we've really established," Bernstein said, "is that anyone who was in the booth could've done it except Kovacs. And the Currys, of course."

"Thank you," Thomas said.

"The only alibi that's worth a damn is Kovacs's phone call in the bottom of the sixth," Bernstein said. "That was checked—wait a minute."

"What is it?"

"There's something wrong." He pointed to the scorecard. "Look at that."

I examined the scorecard closely. Batter by batter, play by play, inning by inning, summary by summary. Then I saw it. T. Graham and Thomas got it at almost the same instant.

"Burdette was pitching a no-hitter through the sixth inning and into the seventh," Thomas said.

"Right," Bernstein said. "He'd given up two runs but he hadn't given up any hits through the end of the sixth. Mrs. Curry may know the rules, but I know the game and the fans. There's no way any fan like Jerry Fielder who was actually scoring the game would break off for a telephone chat while a no-hitter was still a live possibility. A scorecard recording a no-hitter is something you'd frame and put up on your living room wall."

215

Milwaukee Braves vs. New York Mets at Polo Grounds Date Sept. 26, 1962

PLAYERS	1	2	3	4	5	6	7	8	9	10	11	12	AB R H PO A E 2B 3B HR SB Sac HP BB SO RBI
Bolling													
McMillan													
Aaron													
Mathews													
Adcock													
Crandall													
Maye													
Bell													
Burdette													

SUMMARY

WINNING PITCHER _____ LOSING PITCHER _____ INNINGS PITCHED _____ WILD PITCH _____
AT BAT OFF _____ OFF _____ HITS OFF _____ OFF _____ BALK _____
RUNS OFF _____ OFF _____ BASE ON BALLS OFF _____ OFF _____
STRUCK OUT BY _____ BY _____ HIT BY PITCHED BALL _____ RUNS RESPONSIBLE FOR _____

Milwaukee Braves vs. New York Mets at Polo Grounds Date Sept. 26, 1962

PLAYERS	1	2	3	4	5	6	7	8	9	10	11	12	AB R H PO A E 2B 3B HR SB Sac HP BB SO RBI
Neal													
Mantilla													
Ashburn													
Throneberry													
Thomas													
Hickman													
Chacon													
Cannizzaro													
Craig													
Moorhead													

SUMMARY

WINNING PITCHER _____ LOSING PITCHER _____ INNINGS PITCHED _____ WILD PITCH _____
AT BAT OFF _____ OFF _____ HITS OFF _____ OFF _____ BALK _____
RUNS OFF _____ OFF _____ BASE ON BALLS OFF _____ OFF _____
STRUCK OUT BY _____ BY _____ HIT BY PITCHED BALL _____ RUNS RESPONSIBLE FOR _____

216

"So Kovacs's story about the phone call is a lie," I said.

"The timing is wrong," Bernstein corrected me. "The story's inaccurate. The stadium switchboard has verified that a call came in asking for Jerry Fielder to call the stadium operator, and a page went out, and the page was answered."

"Your attention please," a metallic voice said then over the public address system. "Would Mr. Bernstein please call the stadium operator? Mr. Bernstein. Call the stadium operator, please."

"What the—" Bernstein said. "Hey, Terry, find out what that is, willya?"

Terry hadn't gotten very far when Sandy stepped back into the room and said in so many words that we didn't have to bother.

"What do you mean?"

"I placed the call," Sandy said. "I placed it from the telephone at the top of the ramp behind the next booth."

"A light dawns," Bernstein said.

"And before I placed the call, I spent ten minutes in the restroom in the far booth of that section. There were at least half a dozen reporters there, presumably working on their accounts of the game just completed. You can check with them, but I doubt that any would challenge me if I said I left the area ten minutes before I placed the call."

"I think you can fill in 'Yes' under Opportunity for Mr. Kovacs," T. Graham said.

"Of course," I whispered. "He never left the area. He placed the call from the press box phone and then answered the page from the press box phone, knowing that the switchboard operator would never be able to say whether it was Jerry Fielder's voice or somebody else's."

"Interesting theory," Bernstein said. "It'd be even more interesting if there were some way to prove it."

"And if it explained why he stole the sign-out sheet and returned a copy," I added.

"That's it," Thomas almost shouted. "That's what wouldn't come to me."

"Give us a hint," T. Graham said.

Thomas dug into the Legal Research jacket of the Schellenwerk file. He found the slick copy-paper pages of the *Albany Trust* decision stapled together. Flipping impatiently past the caption, synopsis, and headnotes, down to the paragraph just above the text of the opinion, he showed it to us:

> For the plaintiff-appellee: Chadbourne, Wigmore & McCormick, argument by Mr. Nesson, Mr. Mansfield on the brief.
> For the defendant-appellant: Weinreb, Casner & O'Neill, argument by Mr. Fried, Mr. Kovacs on the brief.

"A relic from the days when he was a real lawyer," T. Graham said.

That's why he stole the sign-out sheet," Thomas said. "In the *Albany Trust* case, the guarantors proved that limiting language was typed onto a guaranty contract after one of the parties signed it. They proved that by producing an expert who showed that the pen stroke of the signature went under the type stroke of the limiting language."

"Kovacs was on that case," I said. "He knew that a document examination expert could do that kind of thing."

"Therefore," Thomas said, "he knew that if the police had the original of the sign-out sheet they could tell whether someone who claimed that he'd left before someone else— say, Mary Margaret Fielder—had actually left after she had."

"That's right," Bernstein nodded. "Mary Margaret came in separately from R.J., so she was the last one to log in before Kovacs did. His name was right below hers and their exit signatures overlap."

"I see," T. Graham said. "If the pen stroke of Kovacs's signature went over the pen stroke concededly put down after Kovacs said he left, that would prove that Kovacs falsified his exit time."

"Whereas if the police only had a photocopy," I said, "they

218

couldn't make that kind of determination and wouldn't have any way of challenging the sign-out times. Well done, Thomas."

"The real credit goes to Sandy, don't you think?" Thomas shrugged. "She had the idea of comparing the scorecards and she spotted the discrepancy. And then she was the first one to realize how the phone call could've been rigged."

"I will cheerfully take credit for the scorecard part of it," Sandy said, shaking her head slowly. "But I very much doubt I was the first one to figure out the phone call trick. I do not think Lieutenant Bernstein needed my help to understand that part of the problem."

"When do you think he tumbled to it?" T. Graham asked.

"If one must guess, I would say it probably came to him about ten minutes after the photocopy of the sign-out sheet was delivered to him. That delivery proved that the phone call was either a very unlikely coincidence or a deliberate attempt to conceal guilt."

"You're going too fast for me," I sighed.

"The only really plausible reason for stealing the sign-out sheet in the first place was to protect the murderer," Sandy explained patiently. "Therefore, it was most likely the murderer who sent a copy of the sheet to the police. The murderer's only possible motive for doing so would be to establish a false alibi. The phone call could exculpate Kovacs only in conjunction with the sign-out sheet or the planted scorecard. Hence, unless the phone call was a happy accident that just happened to benefit Kovacs, it was part of a guilty contrivance. Once one realizes that it had to be a trick of some kind, figuring out what the trick was is only a matter of thinking the matter through."

"There, Theodore," Thomas said. "Aren't you ashamed of yourself for asking?"

"I am confident that Lieutenant Bernstein is as capable of that as I am—and he had a head start."

"But then why did he play dumb about that part of it?" I demanded.

"Because none of this impressive logical deduction is evidence," T. Graham said. "And if he hadn't played dumb, he probably wouldn't have had a number of high-spirited civilians for whose actions he could not be held accountable running around gathering evidence in ways that were highly heterodox, not to say occasionally illegal. Would you, lieutenant?" T. Graham glanced up at Bernstein, who had returned to the end section of the press box where the rest of us were still standing.

Framed in the doorway, Bernstein arched his eyebrows and smiled.

"First game of the series,"he said. "Ford against Koufax or maybe Marichal. Who do you like?"

5:23 P.M.

Patrolman Dennis Tippitt sensed trouble the moment he stepped onto the stairs leading to Kovacs's office. He didn't know why he sensed it, but he unfastened the restraining strap on his holster and wrapped his right hand around the grip of his .38.

He moved cautiously up the stairs and knocked on the door to Kovacs's reception area. The door swung open. He started to call Kovacs's name, then checked himself. Through the open door he could see past the reception area into Kovacs's office, and he knew the instant he saw the crumpled body lying on the floor in front of the desk that he was too late to bring Kovacs in. Someone with big and powerful but somehow graceful hands had beaten Louis Kovacs to death.

After September 30

Chapter
Twenty-nine

The document was enormously impressive. The pages were eight-and-one-half by fourteen inches. The paper was heavy, textured bond. Holding the seven pages together was, not a staple, but a brass grommet punched into the upper left-hand corner. Strands of red and blue ribbon led from the grommet to the lower right-hand corner of the first page, where the Seal of the Department of State, stamped in red wax, pinned them to the surface. Stanley Lieberman, Deputy United States Consul in Dublin, Republic of Ireland, had affixed his signature in the lower right-hand corner of the first page beneath a remarkably prolix certification of the authenticity of the remainder of the document.

"It came in this morning," Bernstein said. He handed it to Sandy, who flattened it out on my desk so that Thomas, T. Graham, and I could read it along with her. It was almost five o'clock in the afternoon, October 10, 1962.

"It's just a glorified affidavit," T. Graham muttered. "Dressed up with a little French pastry."

"Deposition on written questions," Bernstein said. "Each question was painfully negotiated. And unless I miss my bet, every answer was written out in advance by an Irish solicitor. All R.J. did was provide the basic information to his lawyer and then read the answers under oath in front of a court reporter."

"Does he admit killing Kovacs?"

"No. Of course, we weren't allowed to ask him in so many words."

"Ah," T. Graham said as he continued to read through the document. "What he does say is that Kovacs was worried about the fact that Fielder had given his scorebook to Sandy, and offered R.J. a thousand dollars if R.J. could retrieve it. Kovacs fed him some cock-and-bull story about the scorebook having wagering information that Kovacs needed."

"I imagine that was enough to make him suspicious," Bernstein said. "After the Saturday Night Fights with the younger Mr. Curry, in the course of which R.J. had his nose rubbed in the fact that the scorebook was critical evidence relating to Jerry's death, he put things together and knew that Kovacs was Jerry's killer."

"And so he killed him," I said. "Why didn't he just tell the police what he knew and leave it to them?"

"That's not why he killed him," Bernstein said. "At least not totally."

"What do you mean?"

"Haven't you wondered why Fielder went to all the trouble to hustle Kovacs with phony inside information on that Mets wager?"

"I can't say I've given it a lot of thought," Thomas admitted. "Jerry was a hustler. A hustler hustles. I hadn't taken it much farther than that."

"And how was Jerry supposed to come out with any money on that particular hustle?"

"I'm not sure," Thomas said. "Kovacs apparently bought

the story and plunged with his own money, but the only way Jerry would've profited from that would've been to bet the other way under assumed names with Kovacs himself."

"That wouldn't work," T. Graham said. "In the first place, betting the other way with Kovacs would have defeated the purpose of the bets Jerry was arranging to have placed to make the phony information look authentic. In the second place, experienced bookies only take bets from people to whom they've been properly introduced."

"So how did Jerry turn a profit on the Kovacs deal?" I asked.

"He didn't," Bernstein said. "All he did was arrange for Kovacs to lose money, and lose a lot of it."

"You've got me," Thomas said. "Why?"

"To punish him. Jerry concluded that Kovacs was the guy who spread the rumors that queered R.J.'s shot at a pro career. Kovacs did that to get back at R.J. for refusing to give Kovacs information about R.J.'s team that Kovacs could use to get an edge in college hoops wagering. Jerry thought that Kovacs deserved to be hurt for doing that, so as a sidelight of the stereo deal he set him up for a major league smack on the wallet."

"That was why Kovacs was at the game that Wednesday night," Sandy said.

"Right. As September wore on, it got painfully clear that no fix was in. No one was taking any dives against the Mets."

"Kovacs no doubt called Fielder," T. Graham said, "and with the shamelessness of his breed demanded an explanation."

"That was my guess," Bernstein nodded, "and R.J. confirms it. Jerry told Kovacs to come to the game that Wednesday night, where Fielder would explain everything, show that he had been fooled as well, and offer some contribution toward making up Kovacs's losses. When Kovacs got to the game, though, Jerry gave him a note that made it clear he'd deliberately taken Kovacs to the cleaners."

"Unfortunately," Sandy said, glancing up from the deposition, "Kovacs reacted to the news that he had been hood-winked by improvising Jerry's murder."

"Which he was able to do," Thomas said, "because we left early."

"And because R.J. left early," Sandy said.

"And most important because Jerry underestimated Kovacs," Bernstein said. "Jerry foresaw the possibility of Kovacs flying into a rage the moment he saw the note. What he didn't think of was Kovacs hiding in one of the bathrooms, confronting Jerry when he could do so safely, killing him, and then using the sign-out sheet and a scorecard he'd filled out himself to concoct an alibi."

"As it turned out," Sandy said, glancing provocatively at Bernstein, "we did not figure all that out quite as quickly as R.J. did. Kovacs died as a result."

"Kovacs got what was coming to him," Thomas said with uncharacteristically brutal dismissiveness. "He took Jerry's life. And he took R.J.'s dream."

"If I wrote the laws," Bernstein nodded, "*that* crime would definitely carry the death penalty. I'm not sure any others would."

Bernstein shook hands with each of us and took his leave. Sandy and I accompanied him to the door of my office. At that portal, Sandy elbowed me in the ribs. I took the hint and let her go alone with Bernstein to the reception area.

I was too far away to hear what she asked him just before he left. But whatever her question might have been, I'm absolutely certain that Bernstein's answer was, "I did it, I'm glad I did it, and if I had it to do over I'd do it again."

226

Epilogue

B y sheer chance I saw R.J. again about six years later. I was in Milan trying to put together a tractor-import loan. The third night there my client insisted on taking me to a basketball game between the Milan Sports Club team and a club team from a little town in southern Italy. The customer is always right, so I went.

R.J. was the star for the visiting team. He was far taller than anyone else on it, but they wouldn't let him play center because that position had to go to an Italian. He played forward instead, and as far as I could see that was fine with him. Time after time he hustled up court, took the pass on the run, pulled up, and swished the ball from nineteen to twenty-three feet out.

I doubt that he would have been more sublimely happy if he'd been canning those shots for the Boston Celtics in the

NBA title game. When I talked to him afterward I learned that he was paid about six dollars a game, his home court served during the day as a live poultry market, and he traveled to away games in an ancient, bone-jarring Fiat bus. But for forty minutes a night during the season, he did what God put him on earth to do.

The next time I really thought about Jerry Fielder, on the other hand, came not too long after the little conference where Lieutenant Bernstein had wrapped things up for us. I was at the Bachelor's Club with three long-standing cronies, getting ready for a couple of hours of bridge. We were just about to start when Frank Gibbon, the youngest member of our group, received an urgent telephone message and excused himself.

As he rose from his chair the other three of us looked at him in understated surprise. I could see he was in an agony of doubt about whether to tell us why he had to renege on this sacrosanct game. Finally, he decided to let us in on it.

"My reserve unit's been called up," he said.

About forty-five minutes later the majordomo wheeled a portable television into the card room, because President Kennedy was going to give a speech. The black and white image flickered on, and the young Irish president explained that the United States Navy was going to blockade Cuba to prevent any more nuclear missiles from being sent there and to force removal of those that were already present; and that the United States was going to do whatever it had to to make the blockade stick, even if that meant an ICBM shootout with the Russians.

"This can't be the real thing," one of the others said. "It's October. America goes to war in April."

He was just trying to break the tension, but the allusion to all those Aprils only underlined the gravity of the crisis. A third of the people in that room would have given you even odds that New York City wouldn't exist twelve hours later.

As I said before, episodes like that help you keep things in

228

perspective. I wondered: With the human race on the brink of annihilation, did it really mean anything that a likable, small-time Irish hustler had risked and lost his life doing what he could to redress a single, grating injustice to one man?

Yes, I decided. You bet it did.